RECKONING DAY

RECKONING DAY

ROBERT VAUGHAN

WOLFPACK
PUBLISHING
—— EST 2013 ——

Reckoning Day
Paperback Edition
Copyright © 2024 Robert Vaughan

Wolfpack Publishing
1707 E. Diana Street
Tampa, Florida 33609

wolfpackpublishing.com

Paperback ISBN 978-1-63977-565-1
eBook ISBN 978-1-63977-564-4
LCCN 2024938892

RECKONING DAY

PROLOGUE

As the stagecoach came down out of the high country and began rolling across the flats, the six-horse team broke into an easy lope. The wheels of the swiftly moving stage kicked up a billowing trail of dust rolling and swirling on the road behind them, though a goodly amount of dust also managed to find its way into the passenger compartment.

"Oh, this dust," a woman complained. "It's intolerable. I don't know how anyone can live out here. Why, I can't even get my breath. Paul, do something."

"Now, Celia, be reasonable," Paul said. "What do you think I can do?"

"You could tell the driver to slow down. Perhaps if we didn't go fast, the dust wouldn't be so bad."

"And we would be so far behind schedule we would never get there," Paul replied. "No, even if I told him to slow down, I'm sure he wouldn't do so. You'll just have to find some way to tolerate it."

The woman was traveling with her husband and

two small children. They were from Canton, Ohio, but were coming west because the husband had accepted a position in a bank.

There was only one other passenger in the coach. She was eighteen, pretty, and an Indian, though she was wearing a dress that was decidedly non-Indian. She took a handkerchief from her handbag, held it under the spigot of the water barrel, and wet it. She wrung it out so that it wasn't dripping, then handed it to Celia.

"This will help," she said. "Hold it over your mouth and nose. The damp cloth will filter out some of the dust."

The woman took the handkerchief and did as the young woman suggested. A moment later she took it down and smiled at her.

"Why, that works marvelously," she said. "Thank you, my dear. But here, you take your handkerchief back. I'm sure you will have need for it. I will use my own."

"It doesn't bother me as much," the young woman said. "I'm used to it." She laughed. "Although I'm somewhat less used to it now than I was. I've been away for two years and I'm just coming back."

"Are you an Indian?" one of the little boys asked.

"Danny!" the mother scolded.

The girl laughed, a soft, lilting laugh like the music of wind chimes.

"That's all right," she said. She looked at Danny. "Yes, Danny, I am Indian. I am Apache."

"Apache? They're the worst!" Danny said.

"Danny!" Celia gasped.

Again the girl laughed.

"I agree, my people are fierce warriors when provoked," she said. "But we can be very loyal friends." She extended her hand. "My name is Yara. And now that I have told you my name, you and I must be friends, for the Apache people do not share their names easily."

"My, how interesting," Celia said. "You said you were away for two years. Where have you been?"

"I was selected from the mission school on the reservation to attend an Indian school in the East. I have been in Pennsylvania."

"Oh, how exciting for you."

"Yes, it was," Yara agreed. "And I saw many wonderful things while I was there. Once, I even got to go to Washington to see the capitol. But I must confess that I am very glad to be coming home again."

"Yes, well, I suppose there's nothing like home, even a place like this," Celia said. She looked through the window of the stage at the vast scenery sliding by outside. "And I must confess, it is beautiful out here in a rugged sort of way." She shivered. "But it is frightening, too. It's so big that it overwhelms you."

"Yes," Yara agreed. "I think I didn't have any idea of the vastness of the territory out here until I saw the way things were in the East."

"What did you learn, Yara?" Paul asked.

"I learned that people are people," Yara said. "Whether they be Indian or white. And I learned that if we live together in peace, we can forge a wonderful future for everyone."

"Have you ever scalped anyone, Yara?" Danny asked.

"Danny!" Celia said, her voice showing the level of her exasperation.

"No, I'm afraid not," Yara replied, laughing easily. "Does that disappoint you, Danny?"

Suddenly there was the sound of gunfire outside, and the coach rumbled to an unscheduled halt.

"What is it?" Celia asked in fear. "Paul, what's going on?"

"I don't know," Paul answered, looking out the window, as frightened as his wife.

"Yara, do you have any idea?" Celia turned toward her new friend.

"No," Yara replied. "Maybe someone is just signaling the driver to stop."

They heard loud angry voices outside, but at first they couldn't understand what was being said. Then, suddenly, a rider appeared just outside the stage. He was wearing a handkerchief tied across the bottom half of his face.

"You folks in the coach," he shouted in a loud, gruff voice. "Come on out of there!"

Cautiously Paul opened the door and stepped out onto the ground. Then he turned and helped his wife down, then the two children. Yara was the last one to get out.

"What is this?" Paul demanded. "What's going on here?"

Celia looked up toward the driver and saw that he was tending to the shotgun guard. The guard's head was tilted back and his eyes were closed. His face was ashen, and that was when she saw the front of his shirt was soaked with blood.

"Paul, that man has been shot."

"That he has, ma'am," one of the two riders said. "I shot 'im." He held up a canvas bag. "I shot 'im for this here money pouch. And now I'll be troublin' you folds for whatever money you have." The outlaw got down from his horse and walked over to them. His eyes were half-covered by droopy lids, one of which was puffed up with a scar the bandanna covering most of his face couldn't quite hide.

"I…I have no money," Paul said.

The scarred outlaw laughed. "Who you tryin' to kid, mister? The way you and your missus and them youngun's are all dudded up there, why, I wouldn't be surprised if you wasn't carryin' more money on you than there is in this here pouch. Now, you can give it to me yourself, or I'll kill you an' take it off your body. Which is it to be?" The man cocked his pistol and pointed it at Paul.

"Paul, give it to him!" Celia insisted.

"It's all we have to live on until we get settled," Paul insisted.

"We're going to Coyote Springs to take a job," Celia said. "We'll get by until you are paid. Give him the money!"

"You better listen to your wife, mister."

With a reluctant sigh, Paul took his billfold out and handed it over.

"There now, that's a good boy." The outlaw looked at Yara. "And what about you?"

"I have no money," Yara said.

"How did you buy a ticket with no money?"

"The Indian school where I attended classes provided me with a travel voucher," she said "That was good for a ticket and meals until I returned home."

"The Indian school?" The rider looked at her more closely. "By god, you are a Indian, aren't you? Look at you, all dressed up like a white woman. And damn near as pretty, too, I'd say."

"Come on, Nathan, we got the pouch and the dude's poke. Let's get out of here."

"Nathan?" Yara asked. "Would that be Nathan Babbit? I remember you from before I left."

Babbit sighed and pulled his handkerchief down. "Turner, you got one hell of a big mouth, you know that?" he said. "And you, girl, you know too damn much." He cocked his pistol and pointed it at her.

"No!" Celia screamed. "Don't do it!"

"Can you give me one good reason why I shouldn't?" Babbit growled.

"Hell, I can," Turner said.

Babbit looked up at him. "What?"

Turner rubbed himself. "How long's it been since you had a soft Indian girl to lay with, Nathan?" he asked. "Seems to me like shootin' her would be a awful waste."

"I don't know," Babbit said. He smiled evilly at Yara. "What do you think, girl? You think you could be nice to my partner an' me if we let you live?"

"I'd rather you shoot me," Yara replied coldly.

"You would, huh? Turner, drop me down that rope. We'll just tie this little ol' gal up an' take her with us."

"You have no right to do that!" Paul said angrily.

Babbit growled. "Right? Mister I got the right to do anything I want, long as I've got this," he said, holding up his pistol.

"But she's just a young girl, an innocent child," Paul insisted.

Babbit laughed. "Mister, there ain't no one innocent."

Turner tossed down the rope and Babbit looped it around Yara, then started to tie her up with it. With his attention diverted, Paul thought he saw the opportunity to jump him, and he did, knocking the outlaw down by the surprise of his action. Emboldened by his initial success, Paul reached down to grab Babbit and administer another blow when Babbit's arm suddenly thrust up. Paul let out an expulsion of air as if he had been hit in the solar plexus. He backed away from Babbit, clutching his stomach. He looked over at his wife with a surprised expression on his face.

"Celia?" he said in a small voice.

At first Celia didn't quite know what happened. Then she saw the bloodstained knife in Babbit's hand.

"No!" she screamed. "No!" She rushed to her husband, who by now had fallen to the ground.

"Papa!" the two boys cried.

Celia cushioned Paul's head in her lap while he breathed his last gasps.

"Milli, I..." he started, then he sighed and was still.

"My god!" Celia said, looking up at Babbit. "You've killed him!"

"Yeah, lady, it happens to all of us sometime," Babbit said coldly. "But I reckon I can send you to him if you want." He pointed his pistol at her and cocked it.

"No!" Yara shouted. "No, don't hurt her! Don't hurt anyone else!"

Babbit lowered the hammer and looked at her. "You'll go with us without no trouble?"

"Yes," she said. "Yes, I'll go without giving you any trouble."

"What's she goin' to ride?" Turner asked. "We only got two horses."

"Ride?" Babbit replied. "Hell, she ain't goin' to ride. She's Indian, ain't she? She can run alongside us. We won't go too fast for her to keep up, and if we do, why, we'll just drag her."

Holding his end of the rope, Babbit remounted, then giving Yara a jerk, started riding. Half stumbling and half running, Yara managed to keep up with them as they rode away. Once, she looked back over her shoulder at the stagecoach, standing still on the road behind her. The driver was looking at the guard, who Yara now knew was dead, while Celia and the two boys were gathered around Paul's body on the ground. Lost in their own sorrow, they didn't even bother to look up as she was led away.

1

The metal bit jangled against the horse's teeth. The horse's hooves clattered on the hard rock, and the leather saddle creaked beneath the weight of its rider. The rider was a tall man with sideburns.

Dane Calder's boots were dusty and well worn; the metal of his spurs had become dull with time. He wore a Colt .44 at his hip and carried a Winchester .44-40 in his saddle sheath.

He dismounted, unhooked his canteen, and took a swallow, then poured some water into his hat. He held it in front of his horse. The horse drank thirstily, though Dane knew the small amount of water did little to slake the animal's thirst. The horse drank all the water then began nuzzling Dane for more.

"Sorry," Dane said quietly. "But that's the best I can do for now. But we'll reach the monastery before nightfall, and there will be water there."

The monastery Dane referred to stood alone in the desert, a testament to the faith that God would provide for the righteous, even in conditions as harsh as this. Records in the monastery indicated that it had been built by the Spanish nearly two hundred years earlier. There were no natural sources of food or water. The monastery garden was supported by irrigation, the water for which was carried in by barrel from a small, not always dependable river, twelve miles to the east.

Except for the members of the religious order who lived in the monastery, no one—Indian, Mexican, or American—lived within fifty miles of the place. As far as anyone could tell, no one had ever lived here. The question then was why had it been built there, and why did the religious order continue to occupy it?

Dane Calder had posed that same question to Father Dominic when he was there once before. With a small smile, Father Dominic had replied, "The answer is a mystery, and the mystery is the answer."

Calder had come to the conclusion yesterday morning that Babbit and Turner were headed for the monastery. It shouldn't have come as a surprise to him. Anyone coming this way would have to stop at the monastery, for there was no other source of food or water within several miles in any direction.

Babbit and Turner were desperate fugitives, men whose faces were plastered on wanted bills all across the southwest. They were wanted for murder and robbery, having held up several stagecoaches and, in the process, killing a couple of guards. The money offered for their capture was five hundred dollars each.

Finding wanted men and turning them over to the law for a reward was Dane Calder's business. Such men were known as bounty hunters. Dane was particularly good at his job…so good in fact that men often spoke generally of bounty hunters, but when they spoke specifically of *the* bounty hunter, everyone knew they were speaking only of Dane Calder.

In the case of Babbit and Turner, however, the chase had gone beyond business. It became personal for Dane when, three days ago, he had come across Yara's body.

Dane knew the girl and her parents, for they were from the same village where Dane had once lived. Despite that, he almost didn't recognize her when he found her. Her body was blackened and swollen in the sun. She had stab wounds all over her body and one of her breasts had been hacked away. It was as brutal and senseless a murder as Dane had ever encountered, and from that point on, the reward money became secondary.

Just before dark, Dane reached the monastery, which was surrounded by high stone walls and secured by a heavy oak gate. When he pulled on a rope attached to a short section of log, the makeshift knocker banged against the large, heavy gates with a booming thunder that resonated through the entire monastery. A moment later, a small window slid open and a brown-hooded face appeared in the opening.

"Who are you?" the face asked.

"My name is Dane."

"What do you want?"

"I want to come in."

"I'm sorry. We can grant no entry."

"But, Brother, I am out of water. You cannot turn me away."

"I am truly sorry," the monk said. "God go with you." The little window slammed shut.

Dane had been here many times before, and he had never been denied entry. In fact, he knew the gatekeeper personally, a man named Brother Tobias. Brother Tobias had a weakness for lemon-drop candy and Dane sometimes brought some to him. He knew then that from the very beginning of their conversation, when Brother Tobias asked who he was, something was wrong. Brother Tobias was trying to send Dane a message.

Dane got on his horse and rode away from the gate.

———

NATHAN BABBIT and Quinn Turner were standing just inside the gate. Turner was peering through the crack between the timbers of the gate.

"What's he doin'?" Babbit asked.

"He's ridin' off," Turner answered.

Babbit chuckled, then put his pistol away. He looked at the short, overweight monk. "You done that real good, padre," he said. "I don't think he suspects a thing."

"I am not a priest," Brother Tobias said. "Therefore I am not addressed as Father."

"Yeah, well, brother, sister, father, padre, reverend, pastor, what the hell difference does it make? All you religious guys are called somethin'. Come on, let's see if the cook has our supper finished. I'm starvin'."

The three men walked back across the little courtyard, which, because of the irrigation and loving care bestowed upon it by the brothers of the order, was lush with flowers, fruit trees, and a vegetable garden. There were a dozen or more monks in the yard, each one occupied in some specific task.

The building they entered was surprisingly cool, kept that way by the hanging ollas, which, while sacrificing some of the precious water by evaporation, paid off the investment by lowering the temperature by several degrees.

"Who was at the gate?" Father Dominic asked.

"A stranger, Father. I do not know who he was," Brother Tobias said.

"And you denied him sanctuary?"

"I had no choice, Father," Brother Tobias said, rolling his eyes toward Babbit and Turner.

"You sent him away?" Father Dominic asked Babbit.

Babbit was a big, ugly man with yellow eyes, a drooping eyelid, and a puffy scar passing through the eyelid and coming to a hook under his nose.

Turner was much smaller, with a ferret-like face and skin, heavily pocked from the scars of some childhood disease.

"He wasn't no ordinary visitor," Babbit said. "His name was Dane Calder, a fella they call the bounty hunter. He's not exactly someone we would want around right now."

"I see," Father Dominic said. "Still, to turn someone away is unthinkable. It is a show of Christian kindness to offer water, food, and shelter to those who ask it of us."

"You're showin' your Christian kindness by takin' care of us," Babbit said. "Now, what about that food? How long does it take your cook to fix a little supper?"

"Forgive me for not mentioning it the moment you came in," Father Dominic said. "The cook has informed me that your supper is ready."

"Well, now, that's more like it! Why didn't you say somethin'," Babbit growled. "Come on, Quinn. Let's get somethin' to eat."

"What is this?" Babbit asked a moment later, when a bowl of beans and a plate of tortillas were set on the table before them.

"This is your supper."

"Is this it? What about that Christian kindness you were talkin' about? You didn't offer us no meat?" Babbit growled.

Father Dominic shook his head. "I'm sorry, in this order we do not eat meat. This is our regular fare. We cannot offer you what we do not have."

"It ain't that bad, Nathan," Turner said, rolling up a tortilla in his fingers and filling it with beans. "It ain't bad at all, and it sure beats jerky."

DANE WAITED until after dark before he returned to the monastery. Leaving his horse hobbled, he slipped up to one of the side walls, then, using chinks and holes in the stone façade to provide foot and hand-holds, he climbed up, slipped over the top, then dropped to the ground on the inside.

Most of the buildings inside the monastery grounds were dark, for candles and oil for lamps were precious commodities to be used sparingly, though here and there a flickering light managed to escape. It wasn't totally dark, however, for the moon was full and bright, and the chapel, dormitory, stable, storage, and grain buildings all gleamed in a soft, silver light like white blooms, sprouting from desert cactus.

The night was alive with the long, high-pitched trills and low viola-like thrums of the frogs. For coun-terpoint there were crickets, the long mournful howl of coyotes, and from the stable, a mule braying and a horse whickering.

With his gun in hand, and staying in the shadows alongside the wall, Dane moved toward the chapel. He found a window and looked inside. There he saw Babbit, Turner, and Father Dominic. Babbit and Turner were pointing their pistols at Father Dominic, who was clutching a chalice and cross tightly to his chest.

"Please." He heard Father Dominic's pleading voice. "You cannot take the chalice and the cross. They are sacred relics, given to the service of God by the King of Spain more than two hundred years ago.

Ten abbots before me have kept them safe. I will not be the one who loses them."

"They're gold, ain't them?" Babbit asked.

"Yes, and you will have to kill me first, if you take them," Father Dominic insisted.

"Well, hell, preacher man, that ain't no problem," Turner said, cocking his pistol.

"Hold it!" Dane shouted. He was still outside the chapel, looking through the window, certainly not in the position he wanted to be to challenge them. But he had no choice. Turner was about to kill Father Dominic.

"What the hell! Where did he come from?" Babbit shouted. Babbit was standing by the one flickering candle, and he snuffed it out. The inside of the chapel was immediately plunged into darkness. Because of that, Dane couldn't see anyone inside. Because he was outside, and lighted by the brightness of the moon, however, he was visible, and both Babbit and Turner fired.

Dane felt a hammer-blow to his shoulder. He returned fire, using the flame pattern from inside as his target. He heard someone groan, then fall. A moment later he heard a crash of glass from the other side of the building and he realized that someone had jumped through the window. He hurried around to try to head him off, but, to his surprise, suddenly found himself growing very dizzy. After that, everything went black.

Nathan Babbit was the one who had leaped through the window and escaped into the night.

Luckily for Dane, Babbit didn't know that Dane had been wounded and was, even then, lying passed out just behind the chapel. Had Babbit known that, he would have finished the job.

Quinn Turner was the man Dane shot in the exchange of gunfire that night, and he died before morning. Even though he was an outlaw who had bullied the brothers and was in the process of stealing their most precious artifacts, they prayed over his body, and buried him, if not in the consecrated graveyard, at least on the grounds.

It was two weeks before Dane left the monastery, his shoulder patched and now nearly mended, thanks to the nursing skills of the brothers of the order. He was leaving empty-handed, for not only had Babbit gotten away, but Dane had no proof that the man he had killed in the shoot-out was Quinn Turner. And without proof, there would be no reward.

Dane was pretty easy about it. As far as he was concerned, it wasn't a total loss. Turner had been one of those responsible for killing Yara Quiet Stream and he was now dead. And though Babbit was on the loose, he was still out there, and Dane was mended and on the prowl again. He had no doubt that he would cross paths with Babbit again someday. In the meantime, there were other outlaws with prices on their head, and Dane wasn't the kind to let his business come to a stop because of one little setback.

2

ONE YEAR LATER

The terrible pain stopped and a warming numbness set in. It was the numbness that allowed Wes Boone to keep up with the others on their mad ride away from the holdup. But with the numbness there also came a weakness from loss of blood, and by the time they rode into the little town of Dust Hollow just before dawn the next morning, Boone was staying in his saddle only by supreme effort of will.

"Hey, Charley, Wes's about to keel over here," Hawk Doyle said. Doyle had taken it on himself to ride beside Boone, and for the last three hours had held the reins of Boone's horse while Boone used both hands on the pommel just to stay up.

"Stay with him," Charley ordered. Charley Redford was the leader of the gang. On the afternoon of the day before, they had hit the bank in Coyote Springs for five thousand dollars.

"Maybe we can find a doctor in town to fix him up," Doyle suggested.

"We don't have time," Charley said. "That posse's goin' to be on us if we wait around here."

"He can't go on much longer, Charley. He needs a doctor."

"He's gut-shot, ain't he? He's goin' to die anyway. Takin' him to a doctor just to have him tell us Boone is goin' to croak is goin' to slow us down more."

"You're all heart, Charley," Boone grunted.

"Yeah, well, we could just drop you off by the side of the road," Charley explained.

"That's a good idea. Why don't we do that?" Morrow asked.

"But look, we got to eat, ain't we?" Doyle suggested. "Maybe we could have the doc's woman fix us some hot grub while he's lookin' at Wes."

"Yeah, all right," Charley agreed. "We'll stop, but just for long enough to get somethin' to eat."

It was still predawn dark, but as the four men rode through the street, their way was lighted by squares of golden light on the ground, cast through the windows of the houses where early risers were already beginning to set to breakfast.

Charley halted his men when they reached the end of the street.

"What is it?" Doyle asked.

"You wanted to take him to the doc, didn't you?

Well, that's the doc's house is down there," Charley said.

"How do you know?"

"I was here once. You know, as I think back on it, the doc's got him a fine-lookin' woman, too. Don't know how an old fool like him got such a young, pretty wife. I seen 'er the first time, I thought she was his daughter."

The house Charley pointed to was a low, single-story building that stood nearly half a block away from the others. A wisp of wood smoke rose from the chimney, carrying with it the aroma of frying bacon.

"Before we ride up there, fellas, take a good look around," Charley said. "Make sure nobody is watchin' us."

The saddles squeaked as the riders twisted to look around. Boone held on, telling himself there was only a short time left, then he could lie down and rest in a nice, soft, bed.

"It looks clear," one of the men said.

"Let's go," Charley replied. He clicked to his horse and the four of them moved slowly across the distance. They stopped just in front of the doctor's house.

JOHN NEWLAND, M.D., the sign read by the door. Charley didn't bother to knock, he just pushed it open. Clay Morrow and Hawk Doyle half carried, half supported Boone inside.

"What the…what is this?" the surprised doctor asked, looking up from his breakfast table. His wife was standing at the stove frying bacon, and she looked around in alarm as well.

"Don't get fretted none, Doc," Charley said. "I'm Charley Redford. I reckon you've heard of me."

"Cactus Charley!" Dr. Newland gasped. "Yes, yes, of course I've heard of you."

Though only twenty-one years old, Charley Redford had already achieved a degree of notoriety as a result of his lawless rampage. His picture decorated wanted posters all over the southwest, and of late, as "Cactus Charley," he had been glamorized as the subject of half a dozen dime novels.

Charley grinned broadly. "Yeah, Cactus Charley, that's me," he said. He was proud of his notoriety, and even though he could barely read, he had a copy of each of the novels that had been written about him. "One of my men got hisself pretty bad shot yesterday afternoon. He needs some doctorin'." He looked over toward the stove. "And the rest of us need some grub."

"What makes you think I would—" Dr. Newland started, then he stopped and sighed. "Never mind, bring him in. Let me take a look at him."

Doyle and Morrow lay Boone on the bed. Dr. Newland sat beside him, then opened his shirt.

"He's lucky," he said. "I don't think there's any festering. But the bullet is going to have to come out."

"Hell, why bother?" Charley asked. "He's gut-shot. That means he's goin' to die."

"Probably," Dr. Newland said. "But not absolutely. I can at least try."

"You want to waste your time on him, go right ahead. Me, I want somethin' to eat. Miz?"

"There's bacon and a skillet," the doctor's wife said. "And a basket of fresh eggs. There's also a pan of biscuits, fresh made. If you want breakfast, fix it yourself. I have to help my husband tend to this man's wound."

Charley pulled his pistol and pointed it at Boone. "Well, hell, if that's all that's gettin' in the way of us gettin' a little grub, I can just put him out of his misery now."

Dr. Newland stepped between Charley and Boone. "If you shoot him, you're goin' to have to shoot me, too," he said.

"All right by me," Charley said easily.

"And me," the woman added, stepping in front of her husband.

Charley looked at them for a moment longer, then chuckled. "All right, have it your way. Hawk, you fix the breakfast."

"Why me? I ain't no cook."

"I said fix the damn breakfast," Charley ordered, his voice flat and cold. "You the one wanted to get Wes tended to."

"All right, all right," Doyle mumbled.

"Doc, you not only got yourself a young, pretty woman, you got a brave one, too," Charley said. "How did an old fart like you get someone like that?"

When Dr. Newland didn't answer, Charley gave both husband and wife an insolent smile and nod, then walked over to join the others at the kitchen stove.

"Here's a little laudanum," Dr. Newland said to Boone, handing him a small bottle. "Take it. You'll need it when I start probing for the bullet."

Dr. Newland's wife assisted him. They removed Boone's shirt and the doctor began digging in the wound for the bullet. Charley, Doyle, and Morrow ate their breakfast as if totally unconcerned with what was going on over on the bed. A few minutes later Newland announced that he had the bullet and he dropped it with a clink into the pan of warm water. The bullet lay in the bottom of the pan with tiny bubbles of blood rising to paint a swirl of red on the water's surface. No one at the breakfast table seemed particularly interested in the medical report.

"You 'bout finished over there, Doc?" Charley asked, coming from the table, carrying a sandwich made from bacon and a biscuit.

"I've got the bullet out."

"Good, get him patched up so we can put him back on his horse."

"This man can't go anywhere," Dr. Newland said. "Why, if you take him out of here now, it'll kill him."

"He knew the chances, just like the rest of us," Charley said. "Wes," he said gruffly. "Come on, Wes. Get up!"

Boone groaned.

"Why can't we leave him here, like the doc said?" Doyle asked.

"We can't do that. He knows where we're goin'. He might talk."

"Boone won't talk," Doyle said. "He's a good man, he won't talk."

"We killed two people in that holdup," Charley said. "That means if we get caught, we're goin' to hang. If they tell him they won't hang him if he'll help 'em find us, are you tellin' me he won't talk?"

"Well, what are we goin' to do," Doyle asked, "if we can't take him with us and we can't leave him here?"

Charley looked at Boone, unconscious now, and sighed. "There's only one thing we can do."

Charley walked over to the bed and picked up a pillow, then pushed it down over Boone's face.

"What? What are you doing?" The doctor's wife gasped in shock. She reached for Charley, but he hit her in the face with a wicked backhand, which sent her careening backward where she hit the wall, then slid down into a sitting position.

"Stop!" Dr. Newland said. "Stop, you're going to kill him!"

"Yeah, Doc, that's what I aim to do," Charley answered with a giggle.

Boone began to struggle beneath the pillow and Charley pressed it down harder.

"Charley, look out!" Morrow suddenly called, and the outlaw looked over to see Dr. Newland fumbling desperately with a shotgun, trying to close the breech.

Charley pulled his pistol and fired, his bullet hitting Newland right between the eyes. The doctor's wife screamed and Charley turned toward her.

"Shut up!" he shouted. "Shut up!"

She screamed again.

Charley fired a second time and the woman quit screaming. A tiny black hole appeared just over her left breast. A trickle of blood oozed down from the hole and her head slumped back against the wall, her eyes open and sightless.

"Damn!" Charley said. "Now look what you made me do."

Outside, and all through the neighborhood, dogs began to bark.

"What was that?" a distant voice called.

"Charley, we better get outta here!" Doyle warned. "The whole town's done been woke up."

"What about Wes?" Doyle asked.

"I'll make sure he's dead," Morrow replied.

"I think those shots come from the doc's house," someone shouted from outside.

"Never mind that! We ain't got time to find out. We got to get out of here."

At Charley's shouted command, the three outlaws bolted through the front door and onto their horses. With the sun showing streaks of red in the eastern sky, they galloped out of town past a dozen or more townspeople, who were, by then, hurrying down to the doctor's house to see the carnage that had been left behind.

THREE WEEKS LATER

"You check the horses?" Charley asked as Doyle came walking back into camp. "They coulda got loose in that storm last night. I wouldn't want to be out here on foot."

"They didn't go nowhere," Doyle said. He sat down on a rock, picked up a stick, and began poking in the dirt. "Charley, how much longer we got to stay out here like this? What's the good of havin' all that money in our saddlebags if we can't spend none of it?"

"I figure that storm last night done us more good than about anythin'," Charley said. "It for sure wiped out our tracks so's no one could trail us. A week or two with no trail to speak of and things will die down," Charley said.

"If we hadn't killed that doctor and his wife, the whole damn territory wouldn't be lookin' for us," Doyle suggested.

"And if you hadn't insisted we get Wes a doctor, I wouldn't a had to kill the doctor and his wife."

"He was hurtin' somethin' awful," Doyle said. "You wouldn't let a horse suffer like he was."

"You'd shoot a horse," Morrow suggested.

"Yeah, well, we'da been better off shootin' Wes and leavin' him on the side of the trail somewhere," Charley suggested. He leaned over the fire and tested the meat he was roasting. "This here rabbit looks about done."

"This is a hell of a breakfast, ain't it? I'm gettin'

damned tired of rabbit, and squirrel and prairie chicken and the like," Doyle growled. "I want a steak."

"And people in hell want ice water," Charley said. "Shut up your bitchin'. You don't want any rabbit, fine, me an' Morrow will eat your part."

"Didn't say I wasn't goin' to eat it. Just said I was tired of it."

Charley took out his knife and started to cut off a piece of rabbit. Just as he did so, however, there was a loud popping sound, then the smack of a bullet crashing into the rabbit. Pieces of the cooked animal flew in every direction.

Charley let out a shout of fear and alarm and jumped back from his demolished breakfast. The other two men jumped up and pulled their guns.

"Just drop 'em right there," a voice called.

"What the hell? Who are you, mister? Show yourself!" Charley shouted.

There was another gunshot and this time the bullet hit the ground right between Charley's feet, then ricocheted up between his legs and whined out over the open prairie.

"I'll aim higher with my next shot," the voice growled.

"No, no!" Charley said, dropping his gun and raising his hands. "We give up! We give up!"

Morrow and Hawk dropped their guns and raised their hands as well.

"That's more like it," the disembodied voice said. There was the sound of boots walking on rocky ground, then a man appeared from behind a rock. He was carrying three pairs of handcuffs and he tossed them forward. "How about you fellas trying these on for size?' he asked.

"Who the hell are you, mister? I don't see no badge," Doyle said.

Charley chuckled softly. "He don't need no badge. Boys, this here is the man they call the bounty hunter. That is you, ain't it? Dane Calder?"

"I'm Calder," Dane said.

"Time was, boys, when Calder was the best," Charley said. "'Course, that was before he run into Nathan Babbit. The way I hear it, he had Nathan cornered, but Nathan beat him in a shoot-out and got away. Is that the way it happened, Calder?" Charley taunted.

"Don't concern yourself with Nathan Babbit. You're the ones occupying my attention now."

"I'm flattered," Charley replied. "Boys," he said to the others. "We should be flattered. The bounty hunter only goes after the best."

"Not the best, sonny," Dane replied coldly. "Just the ones who pay the most. That business you pulled back in Dust Hollow got the dander up in quite a few folks. You fellas are worth five hundred dollars apiece."

"Five hundred dollars apiece, eh?" Charley said. He smiled. "Well, now, I think we can beat that, don't you, boys? We'll give you two thousand to let us go."

Dane shook his head. "Not worth it," he said.

"What do you mean it's not worth it? That's five hundred more than you'll get for the three of us."

"I do somethin' like that, that'd make me an outlaw

and I wouldn't be able to collect any more rewards for scum like you. Besides, it's goin' to be worth five hundred bucks to me just to watch the four of you hang."

"The four of us? What do you mean four of us?"

"Boone's in jail back in Coyote Springs."

"I'll be damned. I was sure the son of a bitch would be dead by now."

Calder took his rope and made three nooses. He put the nooses around the necks of each of his prisoners before ordering them to mount up. As Doyle started to get on his horse he slipped causing a pull against the necks of the other two men.

"Careful there, you dumb bastard!" Charley growled. "You want to break all our necks?"

Once all three prisoners were mounted, Calder tied the end of the rope to his saddle, then he swung up onto his horse.

"All right, gents," he said easily. "Let's head for Coyote Springs."

3

Dane Calder watched the dust rise from the hoof falls of his three prisoners and he thought about the fact that Nathan Babbit was still a free man. Charley Redford had taunted him about it, obviously trying to get a rise out of the bounty hunter. What Charley didn't realize was that he had come much closer than he expected, because the subject of Nathan Babbit was still a sensitive one as far as Dane was concerned.

Dane could not afford to give up everything else just to find Nathan Babbit, but the outlaw was never far from his mind. There was seldom a day that went by he didn't think about Babbit, and whenever he rode into a new town, he found that no matter who he was looking for, no matter what dodger he had in his hand, he was also always looking for a big man with yellow eyes, a drooping eyelid, and a puffed, ugly scar. Dane was tired. It wasn't just the butt-sore tiredness of a long, hard ride. It was the kind of bone-deep weariness that comes on a man after years of riding the trail with one dusty town behind his back and another just ahead.

The bad side of it was it would never get any better.

The good side was that at this stage, it could get no worse.

The anchorless drifting had become a part of Dane's existence. He was a man who had been permanently marked by the saloons, cow towns, stables, dusty streets, and open prairies he had encountered. He could not deny them without denying his own life and in fact had no intention of ever doing so. He was both a long way from home and as close to home as the nearest hotel or back room in a saloon, or even a whore's bed. Most often, though, home was no more than a bedroll made from a saddle blanket and poncho.

"Hey, Calder, you goin' to push us all night, or are we goin' to get a chance to rest a bit?" Charley asked.

"Keep goin'," Dane growled. "We'll be there by midnight."

"Midnight?" Charley complained. "What the hell? You jumped us 'fore daylight this morning". I've heard tell that peace officers have to give their prisoners proper rest, food, an' water."

"Well, there you go, Charley. I'm not a peace officer," Dane said. "Besides, I wouldn't be worryin' a whole lot about rest if I was you. You and your compadres there will be getting an eternity of rest in just about a week or so."

"Yeah? Well, we'll see about that," Charley replied.

"Charley? Charley, you said if we teamed up with you, they'd never catch us," Morrow said. "I don't want to hang, Charley. You hear me? I don't want to hang."

"Shut up, Clay," Charley said. "Ain't nothin' to be gained by whimperin'."

"All of you keep quiet," Dane said. "I'm not in any mood to listen to your prattle."

"How 'bout if I sing a little song?" Charley started. "Buffalo Gals, won't you come out tonight, come out tonight, come out—uhnn!"

The sudden end to his song was brought on by Dane jerking hard on the rope. As the rope was looped around Charley's neck, it had the effect of choking off his efforts.

"Watch it!" Charley said. "You could pull me off here an' break my neck!"

"Really? Well, I wouldn't want to do that, now, would I, Charley?" Dane said. "That would spoil everyone's fun in watching you hang."

"I hate disappointin' all those nice folks like that, Calder," Charley said. "But I ain't plannin' on givin' them a show."

Despite their further protests, Dane Calder pushed his three prisoners far into the night, arriving in Coyote Springs so late that three of the four saloons were already dark and the fourth, though still showing light from the bottom floor, was quiet. The four horses plodded down the dirt street, the hollow clopping echoing back from the darkened false-fronted stores and houses. From the back of one of the houses, a baby cried, and Dane heard the cooing sound of its mother as she comforted it. Such sounds barely penetrated Dane's consciousness. He was aware that another world existed outside his own...a world of husbands and wives, children and homes, schools, churches, and socials, but such things were so remote from his own experience that he was unable even to dredge up a twinge of envy—or regret—for his exclusion.

The jail, like the other buildings in town, was dark. Dane stopped in front and swung down from his horse.

"Ha!" Charley barked in what might have been a laugh. "The sheriff an' his deputies have all gone home for the night. You're goin' to have to bring us back tomorrow."

"You could take us over to the hotel, maybe rent us a room." Doyle suggested.

"Hotel, hell? How 'bout takin' us down to the saloon? We could prob'ly find some whores tha'd share their bed with us tonight," Doyle said.

"Don't know 'bout Calder, though," Charley added. "What self-respectin' whore would have anythin' to do with him?"

Dane tied his horse off at the hitch rail, then stepped up onto the wooden porch in front of the jail. His boots clumped loudly across the boards. His horse whickered, and Dane spun around quickly, his pistol in his hand, the hammer pulled back. Just as he had suspected, the three were trying to ease out of the hitch.

"Hold it, hold it!" Charley said. "We ain't goin' nowhere!"

"Charley, that's just about the first true words you've spoken," Dane said. "You ain't goin' nowhere."

Keeping his pistol leveled at his three prisoners, Dane banged on the front door of the jailhouse.

"What do you want?" a muffled voice called from inside.

"Open the door. I've got some prisoners for you."

"Prisoners? We wasn't expectin' no prisoners. Who might they be?"

"Charley Redford, Clay Morrow, Hawk Doyle," Dane answered.

"What the hell? You got them?" the voice called. Dane could hear footsteps from inside. A key rattled in the lock and a moment later the door opened. A man, obviously roused from his sleep, stood there, wearing boots and a pair of long johns. "Who are you?" he asked.

"Dane Calder."

"Calder? Dane Calder? The fella they call the bounty hunter?"

"You going to take these prisoners or not?"

"Yes, yes, sir, I'll take them," the man said. "I'm Deputy Hank Eubanks, Mr. Calder. Boy, oh boy, is Sheriff McQuade goin' to be surprised come mornin'."

Eubanks reached up beside the door. When he pulled his hand back, it was clutched around a

Greener ten-gauge shotgun. He pointed the double-barrel weapon at the three men.

"All right, you boys, just climb on down real easy now," he said. "I've got a nice room all ready for you."

"These men are worth five hundred dollars each," Dane said. "I'll be needing you to sign a receipt."

"I can't give you no money, Mr. Calder. I'm just the deputy 'round here."

"That's all right," Dane said. "All you have to do is sign the receipt, stating that I brought them in. I'll take care of the rest."

"Yes, sir, I'll be proud to do that, soon as I get these critters locked up. Come along, boys. We got a friend of yours in there, already waitin' to hang. I reckon he can wait a little longer so's you can all hang together." He jabbed Charley in the ribs with the barrel of his shotgun.

"Hey, watch it. That hurts," Charley complained.

"Does it?" the deputy asked, jabbing him again. "Well, now, that's too bad."

FIFTEEN MINUTES later Dane was standing at the bar over in the Silver Horseshoe Saloon.

"Got any Old Overholt?" he asked when the bartender moved down to stand in front of him.

The bartender, who was sucking on a toothpick, nodded without speaking, then turned to pull a bottle down from the wall behind him. He poured a glass and slid it in front of Dane.

"You the fella brung them three in a while ago?" the bartender asked.

Dane nodded then tossed the drink down.

"Seen you comin' in," the bartender said. "Me and Lily there was the only two down here an' we heard the horses, so we looked out to see who it was."

"Who was they?" Lily asked. Lantern light was kind to Lily. Her skin glowed soft and golden and the dissipation of her life didn't show so badly. She managed to look almost as young as her years.

"Charley Redford, Clay Morrow, Hawk Doyle," Dane said, pouring himself a second drink.

"You caught the rest of that bunch?" Lily asked. "All of 'em? All alone?" She walked down to stand beside him. "Karl, pour this man another drink, on me," she said and smiled up at Dane. "It was bad enough them killin' that teller and poor Mr. Eastman when they robbed the bank here. But I heard what they done over in Dust Hollow to poor Dr. Newland and his wife. And the Presnells doin' no more than their Christian duty to succor the wounded. That's one hangin' I don't aim to miss."

Dane took the drink Karl poured, then, with his glass, saluted the woman who had bought it for him. "Thank you, ma'am," he said before he threw back the drink.

4

SIX WEEKS LATER

"All rise!"

There was a scrape of chairs and a rustle of pants, petticoats, and skirts as the spectators in the courtroom stood. A spittoon rang as one male member of the gallery made a last-second, accurate expectoration of his tobacco quid.

"Oyez, oyez, oyez. This court is now in session, the Honorable Frank Sweeny presiding."

The gallery was limited to fifty spectators and tickets for attendance were highly prized commodities. Most people agreed that Judge Sweeny's performances were the best show anywhere, not because of any particular showmanship, but because of his hard-nosed treatment of criminals. He had sentenced so many hardened criminals to hang that he was known far and wide as "King of the Gallows."

Judge Sweeny stepped through a rear door and

viewed his court. He wasn't a tall man, but he was robust, with a square face and piercing blue eyes. He moved quickly to the bench, then sat down.

"Be seated," he said.

The gallery sat, then watched with interest as the convicted prisoners were brought into the room. Included in the gallery were several representatives from the nation's press. Newspapers from San Francisco to New York had capitalized on the notoriety of Cactus Charley of dime-novel fame, and some of the stories openly treated him as a folk hero. Such stories concentrated on the derring-do of the bank robbery and escape, conveniently omitting the details of the murder of Dr. Newland and his wife. The jury, however, composed of twelve hardened citizens of the frontier town of Coyote Springs, was unimpressed by the gang's notoriety. They listened to testimony from witnesses to the bank robbery and from the citizens of Dust Hollow, who reported hearing shots, seeing Charley Redford, Hawk Doyle, and Clay Morrow ride away from the doctor's house, then finding the doctor and his wife dead and the fourth member of their gang, Wes Boone, nearly so. Boone had already been tried, convicted, and sentenced to be hanged for his part in the killing of the bank teller and Ralph Eastman during the bank holdup. In a hollow victory, Boone was found innocent of the deaths of Dr. Newland and his wife.

The evidence was overwhelming and the jury returned a verdict of guilty on all counts. Now all that remained was for Judge Sweeny to pass on their sentence.

"Bailiff, would you position the prisoners before the bench for sentencing, please?" Judge Sweeny said.

"Yes, Your Honor."

The three men were brought before the bench. Clay Morrow and Hawk Doyle stood with their heads bowed contritely. Charley Redford smiled at the judge in arrogant defiance.

Judge Sweeny cleared his throat. "You men have been tried before a jury of twelve men, honest and true, for the murders of Eastman, Adam Brenner, Dr. John Newland and his wife, Elizabeth Newland. You were ably represented by counsel—"

"You mean by an idiot," Charley interrupted.

"By court-appointed counsel," Judge Sweeny went on. "And you have all been found guilty as charged."

"We know all that. Get on with it," Charley taunted.

The bailiff took a step toward Charley, but Judge Sweeny nodded at him, and the bailiff stepped back.

"Additionally, you, Charley Redford—"

"Call me Cactus Charley, everyone else does," Charley interrupted. When the gallery laughed nervously, Charley turned toward them and held his arms over his head, with his handcuffed hands clasped. "These are my people, Judge."

Judge Sweeny banged his gavel several times for order, and when the gallery quieted, he glared at them.

"If there is one more demonstration, I will clear the court and hang these men in private," he growled.

The crowd, not wanting to miss the spectacle of the hanging, fell silent.

"And now, Mr. Redford," the judge continued. "As I was about to say, though you were only tried for those four deaths, you readily admit to the killing of others. Is this correct?"

"Yeah, so what?" Charley replied. "What are you goin' to do, hang me for each killin'?" He giggled.

"If that were possible, Mr. Redford, you may be assured that I would do so. Fortunately one hanging is all it will take. I normally ask God to have mercy upon the souls of those I condemn to the gallows, but for you, Mr. Redford, I offer no such prayer. Indeed, my only regret is that I cannot impose a sentence to be carried out in the hereafter."

"You go to hell, Judge," Charley spat.

"Exactly what I was talking about, Mr. Redford," Judge Sweeny replied. "I am condemning your sorry soul to hell." He picked up his gavel and rapped it sharply against the pad on his desk.

"I sentence Clay Morrow, Hawk Doyle, and most particularly you, Charles Redford, to join with your fellow murderer, Wes Boone, where the four of you will be hanged by the neck until you are dead. Sentence will be carried out at two o'clock on this very afternoon."

There was a buzz of whispering excitement throughout the court as everyone realized that on this very day four prisoners would be hanged.

"Four! Four at one time! This'll sure make a fitting end to all the stories those papers have been carryin' back East!" someone said excitedly.

"Silence! Silence in the court," Judge Sweeny said, and again he slapped his gavel against the pad. The gallery grew quiet. "Deputy Eubanks, escort the condemned men to the holding cells. Court is dismissed."

"Who'll have tickets to the hanging?" the clerk called.

"Me! I want one!" someone called.

"Save one for me!"

The three prisoners, their legs hobbled with an eighteen-inch chain, were chained together for the move back to the cells. As the deputy escorted them out of the court and to the holding cell, they had to move with an awkward gait. They shuffled out as crowds of people pressed around the clerk to get the little blue ticket that would grant them access to the side courtyard where the hanging would take place.

The holding cell was separated from the main jail. It was out in the side courtyard, less than fifty feet from the gallows itself. There, the condemned prisoners would be able to look through the barred windows and watch the crowd gather and the excitement grow as time for their execution approached.

The deputy took them out through the side door of the courthouse, then across the sunbaked, dirt-packed courtyard toward the little holding cell. It was quiet in the yard since, as yet no spectators had been allowed around the gallows.

They passed through the shadow of the gallows. Someone was up on the gallows deck, oiling the hinges to the trapdoor. He pulled the lever and the door swung open with a bang. Doyle let out a little cry of alarm. Charley laughed.

"Don't you fret none, Hawk boy," Deputy Eubanks teased. "They're just greasin' the doors to hell for you." He laughed out loud at his own joke.

"You're gettin' a big kick out of this, ain't you, Hank?" Charley said.

The deputy smiled. "Watchin' you three boys hang is goin' to be like Christmas, New Year's, and my birthday all rolled into one," he said.

"Hank, I sure hope nothin' happens to upset your little plans," Charley said.

Eubanks laughed out loud. "Still makin' the jokes, I see. Well, you may as well enjoy what time you got left. I sure plan to."

"I'm glad I can be so entertainin'," Charley said. He pointed toward the outhouse. "Hey, Hank, before you put us in our cells, how about lettin' me take a leak?"

"You just wait awhile," Eubanks answered.

"Accordin' to what the judge just said, I don't have all that long to wait for anything," Charley replied. "Besides, you want me to pee in my pants? Now, that would be a pretty sight for the ladies that come to see the hangin', won't it?"

Eubanks looked around the courtyard. Except for the worker on the gallows, and Wes Boone, whose face was behind bars in his cell, no one else was in sight.

"All right," he finally relented. "I'll let you take a leak. But be quick about it."

"Thanks," Charley said. "You're goin' to cut me loose from the others, ain't you? I don't care to have them all goin' in there with me."

Eubanks laughed. "Why, Charley, I never knew you were such a shy man," he said. He bent down to unlock the chain. He didn't notice that the man who had been working on the gallows had come down and was walking over toward him. As soon as he was even with the deputy, he pulled a gun and pointed it at Eubanks's head.

"Unlock the hobble chain, too," the gallows worker said. "And get the others."

Eubanks looked up in surprise, then his face reflected his shock. "Why, you ain't Jacob," he gasped. "Where's Jacob? Who are you?"

"I'm the man that's already killed Jacob and I'm gonna blow your brains out too, if you don't do what I tell you to," the man with the gun answered. He smiled, showing stained, crooked teeth. His eyes were yellow and one of them was half-covered with a drooping eyelid. A puffed, ugly scar started on the forehead just above that drooping eye, passed through the lid then under the eye, and hooked around the bottom of his nose. "Now unlock those hobbles like I said."

"Good man, Nathan," Charley said, giggling happily. He looked at the others. "Well, boys, you didn't really think I was just goin' to let us all die, did you? This here is Nathan Babbit, the only man ever to beat Dane Calder."

"I'm real pleased to meet you, Nathan!" Doyle said happily.

"Me, too," Morrow added.

"Charley! Charley, don't forget me!" Boone called from the cell.

"Sorry, Wes. You're still ailin' some from your wound. You ain't quite up to hard ridin' yet," Charley called back.

"You can't leave me here to hang!"

Charley giggled. "Why not? All these people are comin' to town for the show. We got to give 'em somethin', ain't we?"

From behind the courthouse a rider appeared, leading four horses.

"You gents hurry up," the rider urged. "I had to knife the guard at the back gate."

Suddenly two guards came into the courtyard from the front of the building.

"Stop!" one of them shouted. He fired a shot, which missed. Charley, armed now, returned fire and he didn't miss. The guard who had fired collapsed with a hole in his chest. The other guard, suddenly realizing that he was alone, retreated around the corner.

"We've got to get out of here!" Doyle shouted.

"Wait a minute," Charley said. "I got a little business to take care of first." He looked at the deputy and started smiling.

The deputy, realizing what was on Charley's mind,

began to tremble in fear, and he held his hands out in front of him.

"Now, Charley, you don't want to shoot me," he said. "What good will that do you?"

"Oh, it'll do me a world of good, Hank. More good than you'll ever know," Charley said with a broad, evil smile. He raised his gun and fired. A bullet hole appeared in the deputy's forehead, then he pitched back.

"Come on, boys, let's ride!" Charley shouted, swinging into the saddle.

"Don't leave me, you bastards! Don't leave me here like this!" Boone shouted in vain.

By now the shouts and gunfire had alerted the others, and several armed men appeared in the courtyard, just in time to see the five riders gallop through the back gate. They fired at the outlaws but not one bullet found its mark. Nathan Babbit, Charley Redford, and the entire band had gotten away.

5

THAT SAME AFTERNOON

Nearly three hundred people were gathered in the courtyard to watch Wes Boone hang. Many, who had not yet heard of the mass escape, thought they were coming to see four men hanged. When they learned otherwise, there were openly vocal in their disappointment at being cheated out of such a grand spectacle. But they told each other it wasn't a total loss after all. At least one of the outlaws would hang this afternoon.

Enterprising vendors made the best of the situation, passing through the crowd selling lemonade, beer, pretzels, popcorn, and sweet rolls. In one corner of the courtyard a black-frocked preacher stood on an overturned box, delivering a sermon full of fire and brimstone and warnings of perdition.

On the second floor of the courtroom, Judge Sweeny stood at the window of his chambers and looked down on the proceedings. Dane Calder was just behind him, lighting a cigar that he had extracted from a humidor on the judge's desk.

"I told you I'd pay the money and I will," Judge Sweeny said to the man standing behind him looking out the window. "There's fifteen hundred dollars in that brown envelope on my desk."

Dane reached for it.

"The territory will pay another fifteen hundred to get them back, and I'll see to it that the court adds fifteen hundred more. That's three thousand dollars more," Judge Sweeny offered.

"Three thousand dollars?" Dane said, stroking the side of his face. "You know, Judge, with that kind of reward money out there, you're just going to make it harder to find them. There will be too many people trying to get the reward and they'll be getting in the way."

Judge Sweeny turned away from the window. "That reward isn't for everyone," he said. "I'm only offering that to you."

"You're not putting out new dodgers?"

Judge Sweeny shook his head. "No," he said.

"That kind of money is pretty persuasive," Dane replied.

"That's what I'm countin' on. I particularly want these men, Calder," the judge said. He pulled the curtain aside to watch as the hangman checked the single rope that hung from the beam, the noose at its end yawning in grotesque emptiness.

"What about the two fellas who helped them escape? Anything on them?"

"Not more than ten minutes ago Boone gave us the name of one of them," Judge Sweeny replied. "Said he'd tell us the other name if we'd commute his sentence. Of course, I told him we wouldn't make any deals."

"What name did he give you?"

"Babbit. Nathan Babbit."

"Nathan Babbit?" Dane said, looking up in interest.

Judge Sweeny chuckled. "I thought you might be interested," he said.

"Yeah, I'm interested."

"Now, mind you, I can't add anything for him, or the other fella, whoever he was. It's takin' all I've got just to up the ante on Redford and his boys."

"You don't need to add anything for Babbit," Dane said. "Even if there was no reward for him, I'd bring that sorry son of a gun in for free."

"The reward is for dead or alive," Judge Sweeny said. "But if you can, I want them alive. I want to hang these men."

"I make no promises," Dane said.

"You'll at least *try* to get them here alive?"

"I make no promises," Dane said again.

Judge Sweeny stroked his chin for a long moment before he answered. "All right," he said. "I've sentenced them to die. I guess the manner of their execution doesn't really matter. You do whatever it takes."

WES BOONE LOOKED AROUND DEFIANTLY AS he was led to the gallows. He was wearing a gray collarless shirt and gray trousers. His legs weren't hobbled, but his hands were handcuffed behind his back. He squirted out a stream of tobacco juice just as he reached the foot of the thirteen steps, then he hesitated.

"Get on up there, Boone," Sheriff McQuade said. "You done your killin' like a man, now die like one."

Boone turned around to glare at him. "Sheriff, you don't have to give me no lesson on how to die," he said.

"Come on, Wes," McQuade said more gently. "The sooner we get this over with, the better it is for all of us."

Boone moved onto the scaffold, then was positioned under the noose. From here he had a very good look into the faces of the spectators, and he glared at them defiantly.

The clergyman who had been preaching hell and damnation now walked up to the condemned man. "Mr. Boone, do you want to repent?" he asked.

"What have I got to repent for?"

"Why, you have killed, sir?"

Boone looked out over the faces of the crowd. "Yeah? Well, what do you think you people are about to do?"

"The authorities are merely executing their God-given right," the preacher said.

"And the folks here? Is it their God-given right to enjoy watchin' me dance?"

"I beg of you, sir. Repent. Repent now, before it is too late."

"I ain't repentin' for a damned thing."

"Mr. Boone!" the preacher said angrily. "You are goin' to meet God with heresy in your heart and blasphemy on your lips! You'll spend an eternity in hell for that!"

"Thanks for the words, preacher," Boone said sarcastically. "They's real comfortin'."

The preacher, red-faced with anger, turned and walked quickly off the scaffold.

"Any last words, Boone?" Sheriff McQuade asked. McQuade was having to serve as the hangman, since Nathan Babbit had killed the man who was supposed to do the job.

"Yeah. I wonder what they'll be servin' for supper in hell?" Babbit asked. "Whatever it is, it's bound to be better'n that pig swill you serve in this jail."

"I don't know, but when you get there, say hello to a few of my friends for me, will you?" McQuade asked.

"McQuade, you want me to hold you a place at the supper table?" Boone asked as the black hood was slipped over his head.

McQuade chuckled. "That's nice of you, Wes. Real nice," he said. "It's time." He fit the noose. "When the trap opens, don't hunch up your shoulders," he added, trying to be helpful. "Just relax and it'll be better."

"Really? How the hell do you know?" Boone mumbled from under the hood.

When McQuade had him ready, he stepped over to the handle that would open the trapdoor. He glanced up toward the window where Judge Sweeny stood looking down. Sweeny nodded his head and the hangman pulled the handle.

The trapdoor swung down on its hinges and Boone's body dropped about five feet. There was a gasp from the crowd as the body fell.

Boone didn't die right away. For almost four minutes after he fell through the trap door he kept drawing his body up as if in that way he could relieve the weight on his neck. His stomach heaved, and those nearest the scaffold could hear rasping sounds from his throat. Finally his body was still.

"Ghastly business, this," Judge Sweeny said, pouring himself a drink with shaking hands. He looked over at Dane. "You're a fellow who lives your life right on the edge, aren't you, Mr. Calder?"

"You might say that," Dane agreed.

Judge Sweeny tossed his drink down. "Watch your step," he said. "I wouldn't want to ever see you up there on my gallows."

"Don't worry, Judge," Dane replied matter-of-factly. "If it ever came to that…you wouldn't live long enough to see it."

Nervously, Judge Sweeny poured himself yet another drink.

THE SOUND of a shot rolled down the mountainside, picked up resonance, then echoed back from the neighboring mountains. Charley Redford, who was holding a smoking pistol, turned toward his audience of four with a smile on his face. He had just shattered a tossed whiskey bottle with his marksmanship.

"I'd like to see Calder do that," he snarled.

"Charley, there ain't nobody said you ain't good with a gun," Doyle said. "Maybe even as good as Calder, but—"

"*Maybe* as good? Maybe as good?"

"Well, as good then. Maybe even better—"

"There ain't no maybe to it. I *am* better."

"But even if you are, that don't matter. You seen how that sneaky bastard come up on us the last time. He got the drop on us afore we even had a notion he was anywhere around. I say we don't take no chances this time."

"And what do you propose that we do?" Charley asked.

"I think we ought to split up...ever' man for hisself. The cur dog can't follow us all at the same time."

"No, but he can follow just one of us," Morrow pointed out. "And woe betide the one that he follows."

"Yeah? Well, I ain't afraid of Calder," Nathan Babbit said.

"You mean you don't care if he gets on your tail?" Doyle asked.

"Hell, he's been on my tail for more'n a year,"

Babbit replied. "What I ought to do is quit runnin'. I ought to just wait behind a rock and shoot him down."

"You mean you'd shoot him from ambush?" Charley asked.

"Hell, yes. I ain't like you, Charley. I ain't tryin' to build myself no reputation. I don't need to kill him fair and square...I just want to kill him."

"Nathan has a point," Morrow said. "The best way to handle someone like Calder would be to set up an ambush."

"All right, even if that's true, don't you think it would be better for us all to stick together?"

"No," Morrow replied. "I still think it would be best if he didn't even find us at all, and if we split up, we'll have a better chance."

"Except for the one he comes after," Doyle pointed out.

"All right," Charley said. "How about this? Instead of all of us separatin', we'll break into two groups, one of three and one of two. That way he'll still have to make a choice, but even when he does, we'll have him outnumbered."

"All right, I'll go along with that," Morrow said.

"This is the way we'll do it," Charley explained. "Clay, you and Silas McGrath cut out one way, me an' Hawk and Nathan will go another. Now, whichever ones of us gets wind that he ain't on our trail, why, we'll double back and help out. That way we'll have him pinched right in the middle."

"Why that's a wonderful idea!" Doyle said, smiling broadly. He chuckled. "Charley, you shoulda been a general."

6

It was four days before Dane came across a fresh trail. The men he was after had split up, two going in one direction, three going in the other. Clay Morrow and another man—the bartender wasn't sure who the other man was—had stopped in the town of Dust Hollow for a drink, and by the time they were on their way again, Dane had nearly caught up with them.

Morrow took great pains to cover his true trail while leaving false trails for Dane to follow. Morrow and whoever it was with him rode through streams and over hard rock, trying every trick in the book to shake off their pursuer, but doggedly, Dane hung on.

"I didn't figure you was that dumb," Charley said. "Anyway, the way I look at it, Calder takin' out after them like he done just makes it all the better for us."

"Yeah," Doyle said. He smiled. "Yeah, I guess you're right at that. While Clay an' Silas is keepin' Calder busy we'll be runnin'."

Charley chuckled. "Oh, we'll be doin' more than runnin'," he said.

"More than runnin'? What do you mean?"

"You might a noticed that we ain't got two coppers to rub together. Don't you think it would be good to have a little money to do our runnin' on?"

"Yeah, it would be," Doyle replied. "You got 'ny ideas?"

"Nathan seen a bank over in Santo Valle the other day."

"Santo Valle? I don't know the town."

"It's a little flyspeck of a town," Babbit offered. "They ain't got no law 'cept for a sheriff who's so old he can barely get around. That bank's just beggin' to be robbed."

"How much you reckon could be in a bank like that?" Doyle asked.

"Prob'ly not too much. A thousand dollars, tops," Babbit admitted. "But that's the beauty of it, don't you see? If there ain't a whole lot of money in the bank, then they're not goin' to be expectin' anyone to rob it. Hell, they'll prob'ly pee in their pants when we go in. It'll be like takin' candy from a baby."

"Yeah, but if it's not too much money, is it worth it?"

"Well, now, that all depends," Charley said. "How much money you got now?"

Doyle smiled. "Yeah," he said. "Yeah, I see what you're talkin' about."

TWENTY MILES NORTH

"He's still comin'," McGrath said.

Morrow twisted around in his saddle. "How far back is he? Did you see him?"

"Yeah, I got a glimpse of 'im just over the last ridge."

"That'd make him less'n a mile back."

"Ain't they no way we can shake him?" McGrath asked.

"You got 'ny ideas that we ain't tried?" Morrow replied. "We done ever'thing I can think of, an' it ain't even slowed 'im down none."

"So what do you want to do now? You want to wait behind a couple of rocks and shoot him, like I suggested?"

"No, I told you, I don't want to get into a gunfight with him unless the odds are a little better."

"Pretty soon we ain't goin' to have no choice," McGrath pointed out. "He's back there, he's comin', and they ain't nothin' on earth goin' to stop him from catchin' us. Then we're goin' to have to shoot it out with him sure enough, only by then he'll be choosing the time and the place."

"Yeah, well, there is one thing we could do," Morrow suggested, "if you're game for it."

"Hell, I'm willin' to try 'bout anythin'," McGrath said. "What you got in mind?"

"We could split up again. You go one way and I'll go the other."

"Well, now, hold it. That don't make no sense to

me at all. I mean, here you are bitchin' because you say two to one ain't the right kind of odds to go up against him. But you're wantin' us to split up so it'll be one to one."

"It'll be one to one for whoever's trail he dogs," Morrow said. "But the other one of us can get away free and clear. That'll give each one of us a fifty-fifty chance of not havin' to run into him at all. And for whichever one of us that does run into him, well, hell, we won't be no worse off than we are now."

"Yeah, all right," McGrath said, stroking his chin. "I guess them odds is about as good as any. Which way you aimin' to go?"

"I thought I might go west," Morrow said.

"All right, you go west, I'll go south," McGrath replied. He smiled crookedly at Morrow. "I ain't goin' to wish you luck," he said, "'cause if your luck is runnin' good, that'll mean mine is runnin' bad."

"Yeah," Morrow said. "I know what you mean. Maybe we'll see each other around sometime."

"Maybe," McGrath replied. He slapped his heels against his horse's flanks, then started down the middle of a small stream, heading south.

Morrow started west, but after a few moments he reined up and looked back to the point where he and McGrath had separated. McGrath was out of sight now, and because he had gone down the middle of the stream, there was absolutely no sign that he had been there at all.

Morrow saw a willow tree, its boughs hanging low over the water, and he suddenly got an idea. He rode back into the stream, up to the tree, then he reached up and broke off two of the branches. After that he rode back into the rocks, got off his horse and tied it down. He pulled the Winchester from its saddle sheath and bellied down between the rocks, where he not only had cover and concealment, but a good view of the willow tree as well. He jacked a round into the chamber, then piled a couple of rocks on top of each other to make a rest for the rifle. He sighted down the barrel then waited.

When Dane reached the edge of the stream, he stopped. If the two men he was after followed the pattern, they would use the stream for as long as they could to avoid leaving a trail. For most trackers, that ploy would work. Calder, however, could often follow a trail through the water by paying attention to such things as rocks dislodged against the flow of water, or silt, which when disturbed by a horse's hooves would leave a little pattern in the water for several minutes.

Dane was about to check the stream bed when he saw something unusual. There were two limbs broken in the willow tree that hung over the bank of the stream.

That was strange, he thought. In the first place, the limbs should have been supple enough not to be broken by someone passing through them. And in the second place, it would be foolish for someone on the dodge to ride through the limbs anyway. They were close enough to the edge of the stream that they could easily avoid them. It was almost as if they had been broken on purpose.

Dane realized that they *had* been broken on purpose, and in almost the same instant the hair pricked on the back of his neck. Someone had the drop on him. Suddenly, and unexpectedly, Dane threw himself off his horse. At almost the precise instant he made his move, a rifle boomed and a .44-40 bullet cracked through the air at exactly the place where his head had been but a second earlier.

Dane hit the water feet first and ran through the stream, splashing silver sheets of spray as he headed for the opposite side. He zigzagged as he ran, and when the rifle boomed a second time, the strike of the bullet in the water demonstrated the wisdom of his erratic motion, for it hit where he would have been had he run in a straight line.

Dane dived into the tall grass on the bank of the stream, then wriggled on his belly toward the protection of a large rock, about ten yards away. Though he was concealed by the grass, he wasn't protected by it, and a lucky shot would be disastrous.

Dane bent over a large cattail and hooked his hat on top. He found a fairly long branch and used it to hold the cattail down while he backed away from it, moving himself closer to the protection offered by the boulder. When he was as far away from the cattail as the long branch would let him be, he let go and the cattail, with his hat on top, sprang back up to the upright position.

Almost instantly the rifle boomed again and Dane saw his hat go flying. He used that opportunity to move the last few feet to the boulder. There, he sat with his back against the rock and took a few deep breaths.

"Calder? Calder, are you hit?"

Dane recognized Clay Morrow's voice.

"You weren't even close, Morrow," Dane called from behind the rock.

Dane heard Morrow gasp in surprise, for not only was Dane not where Morrow expected him to be, he had also not been hit.

"You bastard!" Morrow shouted. He fired two more times in the vicinity of where he had heard Dane's voice, but the bullets whistled by, harmlessly, overhead.

"Why don't you give up, Morrow?" Dane called.

"Give up? And go back to be hung?"

Dane chuckled. "I'll admit you don't have much to look forward to," he said. "But you may as well know I'm taking you out of here, in your saddle or belly-down on it. Now, which is it to be?"

"Let me think about it a moment."

"Don't take too long," Dane said.

There was a long moment of silence, then Morrow called again. "Calder, you ever thought you might've followed the same trail I rode? Could be you was the one with a price on your head and not me."

"Could've been," Dane admitted, without confessing that he did have a price on his head.

"I mean, when you stop and think about it, we ain't all that different, are we?"

"I don't shoot innocent women," Dane replied.

"If you're talkin' about the doc's wife, it was Charley that shot her."

"You didn't make any effort to stop him."

"No, I reckon I didn't," Morrow replied.

Suddenly, and unexpectedly, Dane heard the sound of a horse's hooves, and when he raised up and looked around, he saw that Morrow had managed to get mounted and was now galloping toward him. Morrow had his pistol in his hand and he was firing at Dane as he rode. One bullet clipped through Dane's collar, coming close enough to take a small nick out of his neck.

When Dane fired back, he saw a puff of dust rising from Morrow's vest, followed by a tiny spray of blood. Morrow pitched backward out of his saddle. One foot hung up in the stirrup and his horse continued to run, raising a plume of water as Morrow was dragged through the stream. As the horse tried to climb the bank out of the water, Morrow's foot disconnected from the stirrup and he lay, motionless, half in the water and half out.

Dane ran over to him, his gun still drawn. When he saw that Morrow was unarmed, having lost his pistol during the dragging across the stream, he holstered his gun and pulled the outlaw out of the water. He was surprised to see that Morrow was still breathing, though the rattle of his breathing told Dane that he wouldn't be alive much longer.

"That was a damn fool thing to do," Dane said.

Morrow tried to laugh, but when he did so,

bubbles of blood frothed out from the corner of his mouth.

"I reckon it was," he admitted. "But there wasn't no way I was goin' to let you take me back to be hung. To tell the truth, I was hopin' you'd shoot me."

"Where are the others?" Dane asked.

Morrow, who had closed his eyes in pain, now opened them and looked at Dane. "You think I'm goin' to tell you that?"

"You don't owe any of them anything," Dane advised him.

"Hell, Calder, I know that," Morrow replied. "That ain't the reason I ain't goin' to tell you nothin'. I ain't tellin' you nothin' 'cause it's the only way I got not of gettin' at you."

"It makes no difference whether you tell me or not," Dane said. "I'll find them."

Again, Morrow tried to laugh, and again bubbles of blood frothed from his mouth.

"Yeah, you prob'ly will. But if it takes you just one day longer, then I figure I'll have my laugh." Morrow suddenly took two or three gasping breaths, then he died.

7

From two miles away Dane could see the little town of Sunstone baking under the sun. It was hot, dry, dusty, and as brittle as a tumbleweed. He had filled his and Morrow's canteen at the stream and kept both canteens for himself, figuring Morrow, who was belly-down on the horse behind him, wouldn't mind.

Even with two canteens Dane had practiced water rationing, but here, with civilization of sorts right in front of him, he allowed himself to drink the final few swallows of one of the canteens. The water was warm, but his tongue was swollen and dry, so any moisture, regardless of temperature, was welcome. And although he was drinking tepid water, he could almost taste the cool beer he would have in the saloon in town.

Dane hooked his canteen back onto the saddle pommel then urged the two horses, the one he was riding and the one he was leading, forward. The buildings in the town had collected the day's heat and were now giving it back in waves, so that Sunstone seemed to shimmer in the distance. A dust devil developed in front of him, propelled by a wind that felt as if it were blowing straight from the fires of hell. A jackrabbit popped up, ran for several feet, then darted under a dusty clump of mesquite.

It took the better part of a quarter of an hour to reach the town, and he rode in slowly, sizing it up with wary eyes. It was a town with only one street. The unpainted wood of the few ramshackle buildings was turning gray and splitting. There was no railroad coming into Sunstone, but there was a stagecoach station with a schedule board announcing the arrival and departure of four stagecoaches per week. He had known many towns like this—isolated, desolate, and stagnant.

Dane rode past the buildings, subconsciously enumerating them as he passed. There was a rooming house, a livery, a smithy's, and a general store that said DRUGS, MEATS, GOODS on its high false front. There was a hotel and restaurant, too, and of course, the obligatory saloon...this one called the Red Star. Across the street from the saloon was the jail. Dane rode up to the hitching rail in front of the jail, dismounted, and patted his shirt and pants a few times. The action sent up puffs of white dust which hovered around him like a cloud. Dane looked up and down the street. A few buildings away a door slammed while across the street, an isinglass shade came down on the upstairs window of the hotel. A sign creaked in the wind and flies buzzed loudly around the piles of horse manure that lay in the street.

Dane pushed open the door. No one was at the desk, but someone was sleeping in one of the bunks in a cell. The door to that cell, like the door to all the others, was standing open. Except for this one, all the cells were empty.

Dane walked over to the wall where several posters were tacked and began studying them. He had left the door to the building standing open, and a gust of wind blew it shut with a loud bang.

"What? What?" the man in the cell said, awakened by the loud pop. He sat up on the bunk and saw Dane standing by his poster wall. "Who are you?" he asked.

Dane looked toward him. "You a prisoner?" he asked.

"A prisoner? Hell no, I'm not a prisoner," the man said indignantly. "I'm the sheriff."

"I got a body for you," Dane said.

"A body? Where?"

"Belly-down across his horse," Dane said. "He's tied up out front."

"Who is it?"

Dane saw a poster with Clay Morrow's name and picture, and he tore it down. "This man," he said.

The sheriff, who was bald-headed and overweight, came out of the cell poking his shirt down into his trousers. "The hell you say. Clay Morrow, huh? He's a bad one. Did you kill him?"

"Yes."

"I suppose you'll be puttin' in for the reward?"

Dane glared at the sheriff. "I didn't kill him for the sport of it," he said.

"No, I don't reckon you did. Well, let me take a look at him and I'll send a wire back," the sheriff said, starting toward the door. "Who will I say is puttin' in for the reward?"

"Dane Calder."

The sheriff stopped in his tracks and looked back toward Dane. "You...you the one name of Dane Calder, the bounty hunter?"

Dane nodded. He held out the posters on Charley Redford, Hawk Doyle, and Nathan Babbit. "Any of these men been through here?" he asked.

"I don't know," the sheriff said. "And the truth is, if they had, I would've given 'em a wide berth. The only job I got is to keep the peace in Sunstone. I ain't in the manhuntin' business. Once I get confirmation on Morrow's body, where will I find you?"

"I'll be in the saloon across the street," Dane said.

Inside the saloon, Silas McGrath was eating biscuits and gravy at a table in the back when he saw Dane Calder push his way through the bat-wing doors. Though this was the first time Silas had seen him up close, there was no doubt in his mind as to who it was. With his size and his hard eyes, the stranger fit perfectly the description Clay Morrow had given him.

For a moment McGrath panicked, and it was all he could do to keep from getting up and bolting through the back door. His hands began to shake so badly that he couldn't hold his fork and he had to put them down on the table in front of him.

"Beer," he heard Calder say to the bartender.

The bartender drew a beer and handed it to Calder. The bounty hunter blew off the head then drank nearly three-quarters of it before he put it down. Then he wiped his mouth with the back of his hand and turned his back to the bar to look out over the patrons.

Damn! He's looking right at me! McGrath thought. He grew tense, waiting for Calder to pull his gun, waiting for the bullet to come slamming into his chest.

But nothing happened.

Calder looked right toward McGrath, then passed his eyes around the rest of the room, showing no recognition whatever.

McGrath smiled broadly. *The mighty Dane Calder didn't recognize me*, he thought. *He's been chasing me all this time and he doesn't even know who I am.*

DANE FINISHED THE BEER, then turned toward the barkeep to ask for another when suddenly something flashed by in front of him. It was a knife! The blade buried itself about half an inch into the bar with a thocking sound. After that, the handle vibrated back and forth.

Instantly Dane drew his pistol and turned toward the direction from which the knife had come. He saw a man getting up from a table with a gun in his hand. However, when that man saw how quickly Dane had drawn, he held his hands up, letting the pistol dangle from its trigger guard.

"No, no," he said. "Don't shoot, mister. Don't shoot!"

"Why the hell not?" Dane growled. "If you would've had your way, I'd be wearing that Arkansas toothpick by now."

"Mister, you're not real, you know that? How did you find me? I didn't leave any more of a trail than a bird would. What does a man have to do to get rid of you?"

Dane chuckled. "The truth is, mister, I lost your trail back there in the stream. The only reason I came into town was to turn Morrow over to the sheriff."

"You got Morrow in jail?"

Dane shook his head. "By now I reckon the sheriff has him down to the undertaker," he said.

"You mean…you didn't follow me here, to Sunstone?"

Dane shook his head again. "I didn't even know you were the one I was after until you tried to stick me with that knife."

"Maybe not," McGrath replied. "But you woulda found me soon enough. The way I figured it, I didn't have no choice."

"You didn't figure it very well. Where are the others?" Dane asked. "Redford, Doyle, Babbit?"

"You think I'm going to tell you that?"

"Why not? As long as you're talking, I'm not shooting," Dane reminded him.

The outlaw smiled, then, slowly, turned the pistol around so that the butt was pointing toward Dane.

"You ain't goin' to shoot anyway," he said. "I've done given up, and this here saloon is full of witnesses who'll swear I was handin' you my gun. You shoot me now, you'll hang."

"Who the hell are you?" Dane asked.

"You mean to tell me you don't even know my name?"

"I never heard anyone say," Dane replied. "All I know is you're one of the two men who helped Redford and his bunch escape," Dane said. "Boone identified Babbit as one of the men, but he didn't tell us your name."

"The name is McGrath, Silas McGrath. You heard of me?"

"Yeah, I've heard of you."

McGrath smiled. "I must be doin' pretty good for Dane Calder to have heard of me."

Until now, everyone in the bar had been looking on in fascinated silence. They had realized that Dane was some sort of lawman who had just found his quarry. But until McGrath said the name, they had no idea they were in the presence of the famous bounty hunter.

"Dane Calder?" someone in the bar said. "Did you hear what he called the man? This here is Dane Calder, the most famous bounty hunter in the Southwest." That was followed by a buzz of excitement as everyone strained to get a close look at the man who had earned such a reputation.

"All right, McGrath," Dane said. "I'm going to park you across the street in this jail until I find the others. If you're real nice to the sheriff, he might feed you."

"You ain't scarin' me none, Calder. This here seems like a nice enough town to me. I don't mind coolin' my heels here for a while. You goin' to take my gun or ain't you?"

Dane started across the floor for McGrath's gun, but before he went half a step, McGrath executed as neat a border roll as Dane had ever seen. He wasn't often caught by surprise, but this time he was…not only by the fact that McGrath would try such a thing, but by the skill with which the man was able to do it.

Dane had relaxed his own position to the point where he had actually let the hammer down on his pistol and even lowered the gun. Now he had to raise the gun back into line while at the same time cocking it. And he was at a disadvantage given that McGrath had acted first.

The quiet room was suddenly shattered with the roar of two pistols snapping firing caps and exploding powder almost simultaneously. The bar patrons yelled and dived or scrambled for cover. White gun smoke billowed out in a cloud that filled the center of the room, momentarily obscuring everything.

As the smoke began to clear, McGrath stared through the white cloud, smiling broadly at Dane. He opened his mouth as if to speak. The only sound he made, however, was a gagging rattle, way back in his throat. The smile left his face, his eyes glazed over, and he pitched forward, his gun clattering to the floor.

Dane stood ready to fire a second shot if needed, but a second shot wasn't necessary. He looked down at McGrath for a moment, then holstered his pistol.

There were calls from outside, then the sound of people running. Several came into the saloon and stood under the rising cloud of gun smoke to stare in wonderment at the dead man on the floor. One of the new arrivals was the sheriff.

"Mister, death seems to follow you like a black cloud," the sheriff observed. He pointed at the body on the floor. "This your doin'?"

"Yes," Dane answered. "I had no choice; you can ask anyone."

"That's right, sheriff, this here fella shot first," someone said.

The sheriff nodded. "He one of the ones you're after?"

Dane nodded. "He helped Charley Redford and the others escape," he said. "In the escape they killed two guards, the hangman, and a deputy sheriff."

"Yeah, I heard about that, even down here," the sheriff said. "Who is this fella?"

"His name is McGrath. Silas McGrath."

"Don't recognize the name. Is there paper on him, too?"

"Yeah," Dane said.

The sheriff sighed. "I just sent the wire about Clay Morrow," he said. "I reckon I can send another one."

"I'm obliged."

"What about the body?" the sheriff asked.

Dane shrugged. "That's your department now, Sheriff. Dead or alive, I turn him over to you. Put him alongside Clay Morrow. They're birds of a feather." As Dane talked to the sheriff he knelt beside McGrath's body and began going through the outlaw's pockets.

"I thought you said the body was mine," the sheriff said.

"The body is yours," Dane replied. "What I find in his pockets is mine. Anyway, you haven't signed the receipt yet."

Dane found a money clip containing twenty dollars in paper currency. In addition to the bills, there were fifteen dollars in coin. He handed the coin to the sheriff. "You can use this to bury him," he said.

"Thanks," the sheriff replied, putting the coins in his pocket.

Dane had not gone through McGrath's pockets for the money, but to see if he could get any clue as to where the others might be. Other than the money, however, he found nothing.

After McGrath's body was dragged out of the saloon and the excitement caused by the event died down, Dane sat at the same table where McGrath had been sitting and ordered a meal of bacon, eggs, and coffee. Back in the kitchen he saw a boy sweeping the floor and he motioned to him. When the boy came to the table, Dane gave him a coin and asked him to take care of his horse. His supper had just been put before him when the boy returned.

"I put up your horse, mister," the boy said.

"Thanks."

"Was he a bad man? The one you killed?"

"Yes," Dane replied.

The boy smiled. "I thought he was. I could tell."

"How could you tell?"

"His eyes," the boy said, moving his fingers across his own eyes. "They were evil. His smile was not happy. He drank a lot and he kept watching the door. I believe he was looking for you."

"I reckon he was looking for me," Dane said. "You have a good eye."

The boy smiled proudly. "Someday, soon, I am going to leave Sunstone and become a bounty hunter, just like you," he said.

"Your mother and dad may want you to wait until you are a little older."

"I have no parents," the boy said.

"Where do you live?"

"Mr. Parlington lets me stay in a nice room in the stable and charges me nothing because I muck out the stalls for him. Mr. Bloss, who owns this saloon, gives me three meals a day because I sweep the floors for him. I have a good life."

Dane thought of his own boyhood and how he had been little more than a slave to his uncle. It would have been much better had he been on his own, like this boy. Others might feel sorry for the boy, but Dane knew that he was serious when he said he had a good life. Dane smiled. "I guess you do at that," he said.

8

D ane had taken a room in the front of the hotel, and the next morning a series of loud popping noises woke him from the soundest sleep he had enjoyed in days. Startled, he sat straight up in bed, slipped his pistol from the holster that hung from the bedpost, then got to his feet, ready for any intrusion.

There was another series of loud pops, followed by the high peal of a woman's laughter, then the sound of a brass band.

Dane moved over to the window and pulled the curtain to one side as he looked down on the street. The street was full of men and women, all dressed in their most colorful finery. There seemed to be a parade of some sort in progress, led by the brass band and a troupe of acrobatic dancers, followed by a highly polished brass fire-engine pumper. The smell of food cooking over open fires filled the soft morning air, and Dane decided he would go down to have breakfast and to see what was going on.

Fifteen minutes later he was eating a bacon-and-biscuit sandwich as he watched the celebration. When the sheriff saw Dane, he smiled and come over to him.

"I haven't been keeping up with the date," Dane said. "Is it the Fourth of July?"

The sheriff laughed. "The Fourth of July? No, that was two months ago."

"Really? Then what's the celebration?"

"Why, you're the cause of our celebration," the sheriff replied. "You mean you haven't figured that out yet?"

"What the hell are you talking about? How am I the cause of your celebration?"

"I take it you haven't gone down to look at the display on the porch of the general store?" the sheriff asked.

"No."

"Go take a look, Mr. Calder. I think you'll be proud."

Finishing his biscuit, Dane walked down toward the general store. There were several people—men, women, and children—standing around the front porch looking at whatever it was the sheriff said was displayed there. When Dane got closer, he drew in a sharp breath of surprise.

There, in a pair of wooden coffins standing up against the wall, were the bodies of Clay Morrow and Silas McGrath. Both outlaws were dressed in black suits and their arms were crossed across their chests. Morrow held a pistol in his right hand and nothing in his left. McGrath clutched a pistol in his left hand while in his right he held the knife he had thrown at Dane. Morrow's eyes were closed, but McGrath's were open, though the left eyelid was half-closed. McGrath's mouth was closed, but Morrow's was open in what appeared to be a snarl. Dane had killed both men with bullets to the heart. Because of that, their wounds weren't visible.

"It's the bounty hunter!" someone shouted, noticing Dane looking at the bodies.

"The bounty hunter!"

"Three cheers for Dane Calder!" someone else called. "Hip, hip…"

"Hooray!"

"Hip, hip…"

"Hooray!"

"Hip hip…"

"Hooray!"

Dane held up his hand to silence them, then walked up for a closer look at a hand-lettered sign propped up at the foot of the coffins:

> *Here are the bodies of the bandits*
> *Clay Morrow and Silas McGrath, killed*
> *by the Bounty Hunter, Dane Calder.*
> *The Gunfights that killed the two men*
> *took placeright here in Sunstone.*

"This is going to make our town very famous," someone said, and when Dane looked around, he saw the young boy who had stabled his horse for him the night before. "Of course, everyone knows that

Morrow wasn't really killed here, but we have his body and the sheriff says that is the same thing."

"Is that what everyone thinks?" Dane asked. "That this is going to make Sunstone famous?"

"Yes. The sheriff said that now everyone will come to see where the gunfights happened. They'll buy drinks and meals in the saloon and they'll stay in the hotel. The sheriff says everyone will get rich because of this."

"And that's what all this is about? This parade and picnic?"

"Yes," the boy replied. "The sheriff says we'll have such a celebration every year at this time. It would be nice if you could come every year."

"Sure. And maybe I could kill someone new for you next year," Dane suggested.

"Do you think so? That would really be good," the boy said enthusiastically, not picking up on Dane's sarcasm.

Dane shook his head slowly, then started toward the stable. The sooner he could get out of this town, the better.

"For you, Mr. Calder, there is no charge," the liveryman said when Dane reclaimed his horse. "You have made our town famous."

"Yeah, so I noticed," Dane growled.

"You're always welcome here, Mr. Calder," the liveryman called as Dane rode away. Dane didn't answer.

Dane didn't enjoy killing, but it wasn't something he backed away from. In any life-and-death confrontation, he knew he must be prepared to kill without hesitation if need be.

There had been strong reactions to his killing before. Friends or close relatives of his victims had sworn revenge, and more than one of them had come close to carrying out their vow. And though, as a bounty hunter Dane was always acting within the guidelines of the law, those guidelines were so thinly drawn that sometimes a misunderstanding of his role put him afoul of the law. On more than one occasion he had nearly fallen victim to the same law he was serving, when an overzealous peace officer would charge him with murder. He was, in fact, still a wanted man in some parts of the West, including one old, still-outstanding warrant from Montana, where, on one terrible night, he had fought his drunken uncle, the same uncle who had nearly enslaved him, to keep the man from raping his own daughter. It was during that fight Dane killed his first man. That man was his uncle, and Dane had killed him in self-defense. Even so, a warrant was issued, charging Dane with murder, and Dane knew that he could never go back and make the authorities believe what really happened.

Dane left home on the run and he had been on the run ever since. He lived with the Apaches long enough to adapt himself to their ways, even to being adopted as a blood brother by some of the Apache leaders. He was born with courage and a fierce will. From his blood brothers he learned scouting, tracking, and surviving. Those were exactly the skills that would serve him well in his chosen field of bounty hunter. His phenomenal success in his profession had earned him the reputation that now honored and sometimes plagued, him.

In Dane's trade, he had received expressions of gratitude before. This was especially true in the case of relatives of the victims the outlaws Dane encountered. But never before had an entire town put his victims on public display and thrown a town party to celebrate. It was more than he could stomach, and he couldn't wait to shake the dust of this town from his feet. As soon as he was out of Sunstone, he put his horse into a ground-eating lope, placing as much distance behind him as he could.

9

Santo Valle was a small town, just as Nathan Babbit had said. However, because it was the only town within a radius of fifty miles, it was a busy town, and half a dozen wagons were parked along the streets. The board sidewalks were full of men and women, farmers and ranchers, looking in the windows of the shops, hurrying to and fro.

"What the hell?" Charley said, surprised by the number of people. "Is this Saturday?"

"I don't know, I don't keep no calendar," Babbit answered.

"There's an awful lot of people in town, Charley," Doyle said. "Maybe too many."

"Yeah?" Hawk answered. "Well, look at 'em. Most of 'em ain't wearin' guns. Don't worry about it."

"There's the bank over there," Babbit said as he pointed out the building.

The bank was a rather flimsy-looking building, thrown together from ripsawed lumber and leaning so that it looked as if a good, stiff wind would knock it over. Hawk chuckled when he saw it.

"Hell, we don't have to rob this bank, boys. We can just kick it down," he said.

"Let's do it and be gone," Babbit said.

"Wait a minute, wait a minute," Charley said, holding up his hand. "Let's take a ride up and down the street first, just to get our bearings."

"Good idea," Doyle said, breathing a sigh of relief.

"Hawk, you take the left side. Count everybody you see carryin' a gun. Nathan, you take the right."

The three men rode slowly down the entire length of the town, then they turned their horses and rode back.

"I seen three that was wearin' guns," Doyle said.

"I only seen one on my side," Babbit added.

"Any of them look like they knew how to use them?"

"The old fart on my side looked like he didn't even have the strength to pull his gun out of the holster, let alone use it," Babbit said.

"Hawk?"

"No," Doyle answered. "They didn't any of 'em look like they knew much more'n which end of the gun the bullet comes out."

Charley smiled. "Well, then, boys, let's go get us a little travelin' money. Hawk, you stay outside with the horses."

Charley and Babbit swung down from their horses and handed the reins over to Doyle, who stayed mounted. He held the reins of all three horses with his left hand while in his right he held his pistol, though he kept it low and out of sight.

As soon as Charley and Babbit were inside, they pulled their pistols.

"This is a holdup!" Charley shouted. "You, teller, empty out your bank drawer and put all the money in a bag!"

Nervously the teller began to comply, emptying his drawer in just a few seconds.

"Is that all there is? There can't be more'n a couple hundred there," Charley said in disbelief.

"That's all there is," the teller insisted.

Charley took the sack. "I want to see what you've got in the safe," he demanded.

"The hell you say! You ain't gettin' any more money from this bank!" a customer suddenly shouted.

Charley swung his gun toward the customer, who was also armed. The customer fired first. His bullet hit an inkwell on one of the tables, sending up a spray of ink. Charley returned fire and his bullet found its mark. Nathan fired toward the teller's window and his bullet shattered the shaded glass around the teller cages. Another customer in the bank fired and Babbit returned fire, killing him.

"Let's get the hell out of here!" Charley shouted.

Outside the bank, the townspeople, hearing the shots, realized at once what was going on.

"The bank!" someone shouted. "They're robbin' the bank!"

"Charley, Nathan!" Doyle shouted. "Get out of there! Fast!"

One of the armed townspeople started running toward the bank with his pistol drawn. Doyle shot him, dropping him in the middle of the street. Until that moment not everyone realized that Doyle, too, was one of the bank robbers. Seeing that he was one of them, the townspeople began screaming and running for cover.

Clutching the canvas bag in his left hand, Charley and Babbit backed out of the bank. Babbit fired three more shots into the bank, knocking out the windows on both sides and in the door.

"Get mounted!" Doyle called, holding the reins down for his two partners.

Across the street a young store clerk, no more than a boy, came running out of the store, wearing his apron and carrying a boom in one hand and a rifle in the other. He dropped the broom, raised the rifle, and fired at the three robbers. His bullet hit Doyle in the side, and with a roar of pain and anger, Doyle fired back, killing the boy. From the front porch of a hardware store, a man fired both barrels of a shotgun, but his gun was loaded with light birdshot and he was too far away to be effective. The pellets peppered and stung, but none of them penetrated the skin.

Babbit grabbed the horse nearest him and swung into the saddle. When the owner stepped out the door of a nearby shop to protest, Babbit shot at him, and the bullet, hitting the door frame right beside the man's head, drove him back inside.

The sheriff, an older man just as Babbit had described him, was just now reaching the scene, having run the entire length of the street from the sheriff's office. He was carrying a rifle and he raised it to his shoulders.

"You fellas stop right there!" he called.

"Would you look at that old fool?" Charley laughed, shooting the sheriff right between the eyes. His bullet came out of the back of the man's skull, carrying with it a little spray of blood, bone, and brain matter.

The three robbers rode toward the end of town only to see a dozen or more of the townspeople rolling a wagon into the street. The townspeople then tipped the wagon over as a barricade and gathered behind it, all of them armed and ready.

"Charley, we can't go that way!" Doyle shouted.

"This way!" Charley yelled, turning off the street and leading them through a churchyard where a funeral was in progress and the body was just being carried from the church. At the sound of gunfire and the sight of three mounted and armed men bearing down on them, the funeral procession broke up amid screams and shouts of terror and outrage. The pall-bearers dropped the coffin and the lid popped off, allowing the last remains of a bearded old man to roll out.

By the time the townspeople regrouped and mounted, Charley Redford, Hawk Doyle, and Nathan Babbit had a two-mile lead on them. With the sheriff dead and no effective leader to organize them, the pursuit only lasted for a few miles. After that the men gave up and came back to town to help calm the fears and bury the dead.

"THEY'VE STOPPED CHASIN' us," Charley said, looking back over his shoulder. "We can give the animals a blow now."

The three riders reined up, then swung down from their saddles and began walking their horses. Doyle, who had been hit in the hip, was walking with a painful limp. There was blood on the front of his trousers.

"You bad hit, pard?" Charley asked solicitously.

"No."

"You sure? You're covered with blood and you got a pretty bad hitch-along in your get-about there."

"I ain't hurt bad," Doyle insisted. "I got a bullet in my hip, but it didn't hit none of my vitals."

"Yeah, well, we can't leave the bullet in there," Charley said. "We'll have to get you to a doctor somewhere."

"No!" Doyle shouted. "I seen how you got a doctor for Boone. I ain't plannin' on lettin' you leave me somewhere to die."

"That was different," Charley said. "We was on the run then."

"Well, what the hell, Charley? We ain't exactly goin' to a ball now."

Charley and Babbit laughed.

"That's the truth," Charley said. "All right, if you

think you can keep up with us, go ahead. But you start slowin' us down any, we're goin' to leave you."

"I didn't figure it would be any otherwise," Doyle replied.

"You want, I can get that bullet out for you," Babbit offered.

"You a doctor, are you?"

"I've took out a few bullets in my day," Babbit said, "and some of 'em lived."

"I'll pass on that offer, but thanks just the same," Doyle said.

Despite Doyle's brave protestations, by nightfall the pain was almost unbearable and he knew he wouldn't be able to go on unless the bullet was removed. He finally spoke the words.

"Nathan," he said thickly. "You serious 'bout bein' able to take out a bullet?"

Babbit chuckled. "You ready for it to come out now, are you?"

"Yes."

"I thought you would be. I've heard 'em talk brave before, but most always they change their mind. I'll take it out for you."

"Thanks."

"It's goin' to cost you."

"Cost me? Cost me what?"

"Your share of the money we took from the bank."

"Are you crazy? I got shot for that money. You think I'm goin' to give it to you?"

"Don't look to me like you got no choice," Babbit

said. "Anyhow, what's the big deal. We only got a hundred fifty dollars. Your share's just fifty bucks."

"Who would've thought they would put up such a fight for just a hundred fifty dollars?" Doyle asked. "Four men killed, me wounded, all for a lousy hundred fifty dollars."

"Do we have a deal?" Babbit asked.

At that very moment a wave of nauseating pain swept over Doyle with such intensity that it was all he could do to stay in the saddle. "All right, you bastard, all right, we have a deal. You can have my share, just get the damn bullet out," Doyle said in a strained voice.

"I know this country, Charley," Babbit said. "Head up into that draw over there. That'll take us into Snake Canyon."

"Good," Charley said. "Maybe we can hole up for a while."

"We're goin' to hole up?" Doyle asked.

"That's right, Hawk, we're goin' to hole up," Charley said. He chuckled. "Did you really think we was goin' to leave you?"

"I don't know," Doyle answered. "Yeah, I guess I thought you might."

"Well, we ain't. We're the only ones left now. That means we got to stick together. Besides, what would folks think of Cactus Charley if they knew he abandoned his friends?"

"Yeah," Doyle replied, thinking of Wes Boone, Clay Morrow, and Silas McGrath. "Yeah, what would they think of you?"

It was another hour of painful riding before they stopped. Doyle climbed down from his horse, removed the saddle, then lay down, using it as a pillow. The pain, which had been localized in his hip, now spread throughout both legs and up his back.

"We need to build us a fire," Babbit said.

"Kind of hate to," Charley said. "You can see a fire a long way off at night. Somebody might see this and get to wonderin' who's out here."

"We got to have a fire for me to heat the knife," Babbit said.

There was the double, metallic click of a pistol being cocked, and when Babbit and Charley looked around, they saw that Doyle was pointing his gun at Charley.

"Let him build a fire, Charley," Doyle said through clenched teeth. "Else he'll have to be takin' a bullet outta both of us."

"Sure, Hawk, sure," Charley said, holding his hands up. "I didn't say we wasn't goin' to build one. I was just pointin' out that we needed to be extra careful, that's all. Go ahead, Nathan, build your fire."

Doyle, no longer having to fight to stay alert and in the saddle, drifted in and out of consciousness. He was aware of Nathan Babbit gathering bits of mesquite wood, but he didn't see him actually start the fire. He saw the golden bubble of light in the night, with Charley and Babbit silhouetted against the flames, then he passed out again.

He woke up again when Babbit started actually digging for the bullet. The pain was excruciating, much more intense than it had been at any time before. He passed out again. When he came through the next time, Babbit was holding the bloodied bullet between his fingers and smiling broadly, his eyes and teeth glowing orange red in the snapping fire.

"Can you believe this?" Babbit said. "This here is a twenty-two. Who shot you anyway, Hawk? Some kid with a toy gun?"

"I don't remember," said Doyle, who, in fact, did recall at that moment the young, apron-clad boy he had killed.

"Give me three of your bullets," Babbit said.

"What? What do you want my bullets for?"

"Because I need the gunpowder," Babbit replied. "And I ain't plannin' on usin' any of my own."

"I got a box of cartridges in my saddlebag," Doyle said. He tried to reach for them but was too weak.

"I'll get 'em," Babbit offered generously. When he opened the box, he took out ten or twelve, dropping the extra cartridges into his own pocket. He came back to sit beside Doyle as he separated the bullets from the cartridges. When he had all three separated, he poured the powder on the wound.

"What's that for?" Doyle asked.

"You'll see," Babbit replied. Without a word of explanation, he picked up a burning brand from the fire and touched off the powder. It made a white-hot flash.

Doyle had time only for a gasp of pain before he passed out.

10

When Doyle opened his eyes the next morning, he was looking directly at the campfire, or rather at what had been the camp fire. Now there were only a few white coals with a tiny wisp of smoke curling up from the ashes.

"Charley," he said. "Charley, could I have a drink of water?"

When no one answered, Doyle turned, with a great effort, to look around. He didn't see anyone.

"Charley? Nathan?" he shouted, the effort of the yell causing his wound to throb.

There was still no answer.

With a supreme effort Doyle sat up and looked around. The camp was totally deserted. Not only were Charley and Babbit gone, but all three horses were as well. They had left in the night, leaving him wounded and without a mount.

"You bastard!" Doyle shouted. He picked up a rock and threw it, though the effort caused pain to shoot through him like a hot knife. He fell back down and lay there until the pain subsided, somewhat. The thirst he had awakened with seemed to increase with his efforts, so he reached for his canteen. When he couldn't find it on his saddle pommel, he looked around for it.

The canteen was gone. So were his saddlebags. There was jerky, raisins, and dried beans in his saddlebag. Not only had they taken his horse, they had taken his canteen and his food.

Waves of panic swept over him, pushing aside his rage and even the pain. He was abandoned out here, no horse, too wounded to walk, no food, and no water. He was going to die, a long, slow, agonizing death. *Even Wes had it better than this*, he thought. *He had food, water, and a place to sleep, followed by a quick death.*

"Damn!" he shouted into the dry, morning wind. "I would have been better off lettin' them hang me."

Doyle saw his pistol and, in a sudden impulse, drew it from his holster. He put the barrel to his temple.

"Charley Redford! Nathan Babbit!" he shouted. "I'll be waiting for you in hell!"

Doyle pulled the trigger.

It was that same afternoon when Dane, who had been alone on the range for the last two days and so knew nothing of Charley Redford's most recent bank robbery, pushed through the bat-wing doors of the Gilded Lily Saloon in the little town of Three Wells. It was still too early in the day for the evening trade. As a result an empty beer mug and a half-full ashtray conveniently placed by the piano provided the only evidence that anyone ever played the instrument. Dane ordered a beer, and when it was served, he turned around to survey the room as he drank it.

Two people were sitting at the table nearest the piano...a middle-aged cowboy and the only bargirl who was working at this hour. The fact that both of them had only one glass before them, and that glass was still half-full, indicated that the bargirl either found the cowboy's company pleasant or had accepted the slowness of the afternoon.

There were a few people sitting at one of the other tables and a lively card game was in progress. The table was crowded with brightly colored poker chips and empty beer mugs. There were two brass spittoons within spitting distance of the players, but despite their presence, the floor was riddled with expectorated tobacco quids and chewed cigar butts.

Suddenly one of the players threw his cards on the table in disgust, then stood up. "I've had it boys," he said. "This is the unluckiest chair I've ever sat in. I ain't drawed a winnin' hand all night."

Another player looked over toward the bar and saw Dane watching them.

"We have an empty chair here, mister, if you'd care to sit in."

Dane tossed the rest of his drink down, then

wiped the back of his hand across his mouth. He had learned long ago that it was sometimes easier to pick up information through casual conversation over a few drinks and a deck of cards than to ask outright. Maybe someone at the table had heard something about Redford and the others. That was justification for joining the card game, though in truth he did enjoy a good game now and then.

"Thanks for the invite," Dane said. "I will join you if you don't mind."

"What you take out of your pocket and put in front of you is all the money you can play with," one of the men said. "You can't go back for more."

"And you can't put any more in front of you than the most any of us have."

"Who's been the winner so far?"

"That'd be the doc here," one of the cowboys said. "You'd better watch out for him. He's pretty good at the game."

"Thanks for the warning. And you would be the doc?" Dane asked, addressing the man with the largest pile of money.

"I am," the tall, thin, cadaverous-looking man replied. He was wearing a black suit, a shoestring tie, and a flat-crown, black hat. He counted the money in front of him. "I've got forty-five dollars here."

Dane bought forty-five dollars' worth of chips and stacked them up in front of him.

"You just passin' through Three Wells?" the man in black asked as he dealt the cards. It was easy to see why he was ahead. He handled the cards easily, gracefully, whereas the others around the table looked awkward even, picking up the pasteboards.

"Depends," Dane answered.

"On what?" one of the other men asked.

"On how much I win here. If I win enough, I might buy a ranch and some cattle, get married, settle down, raise a family, join a church, run for the city council, and become a substantial citizen."

The men around the table laughed out loud.

"Say, Smokey," Doc called to the cowboy who was sitting with the bar girl. "Did you hear this fella? If he wins big, he's goin' to be lookin' for a wife. You better hang on to Belle while you can."

Belle looked over at Dane. "Honey, you're a good-lookin' man," she teased. "You wouldn't have to win too much to get me."

Belle's good-natured response brought more laughter.

Dane won the first hand.

"Better watch it, Doc," one of the cowboys said. "This fella's on his way."

The game continued for several hands. Dane was winning a little more than he was losing, but he wasn't the big winner. Neither was the one called Doc at this point, the play of Dane changing the dynamics to the point where everyone seemed to be about even. This had the effect of improving everyone's mood and the talk came freely. Besides Dr. Andrews, who was a real doctor in addition to being an almost professional gambler, the other men in the game were Louis Phillips, a small rancher, Ken Zetlermoyer, a leathersmith, and Matt Woolsey, who owned the feed-and-seed store.

"Say," Dane said as if merely taking part in the conversation, "did any of you fellas hear about the big jailbreak they had over in Coyote Springs a few weeks ago?"

"Jailbreak? Mister, that's old news. Where you been?" Louis replied. "Hell, yesterday Charley Redford and his boys done robbed 'em a bank over in Santo Valle."

"Some bank robbery," Ken said in disgust. "They only made off with one hundred and fifty dollars."

"They didn't get much money, that's true," Matt agreed. "But they killed four people doin' it. One of 'em was just a boy."

"A boy?" Doc asked. "What boy? I've doctored a few of the young'uns over there."

"It was Muley Simpson's boy," Matt replied. "Muley runs the general store there, you know, and his boy was workin' for him. Seems the boy had just got hisself a new twenty-two rifle, an' when all the shootin' started, why, he run out onto the front porch an' joined in the melee. They say he hit one of 'em, though they might just be sayin' that to ease Muley's pain some. Whether he actual did hit one of them or not, he got their attention, 'cause he was shot dead, right there on the front porch of his pa's store."

"That's a damned shame. It's too bad they didn't get all them fellas hung when they had the chance," Ken said. "I wonder where they are now?"

"Say, you know, I was talkin' to one of my

nighthawks this mornin'," Louis said. "Well, it was Ned Wells, you fellas all know him. Anyhow, I was talkin' to him an' he said that last night he thought he saw a campfire down in Snake Canyon. I didn't put much store in it at the time, but now that I think back on it, don't it seem to you a little curious? I mean why would anyone want to go in there? The place is so desolate that a hawk has to carry a lunch just to fly over."

The others laughed.

"Snake Canyon, eh?" Ken said. "You think maybe Charley Redford and his bunch is holed up there?"

"Well, if I was on the run, that's sure where I'd go," Louis said. "Why, they's enough draws and gullies in that place to hide a whole army."

As the evening progressed several more people came in, until eventually the saloon was noisy and crowded with its evening customers. Three of the most noticeable of the newly arrived customers were young men who wore their guns strapped low. They were louder and more boisterous than anyone else in the establishment, and they made a lace for themselves at the bar by elbowing others out of the way. Occasionally one of them would get off a joke at someone else's expense, and he and the other two would laugh uproariously at his cleverness, unaware, or unconcerned, that the rest of the people in the saloon were not laughing with them, but were, instead, taking it all in, in embarrassed silence.

"Who are the funny boys?" Dane finally asked.

"The one with blond hair and the loudest mouth is

Eli Stone. He's the oldest. The one with the red hair is Fred Taylor. The one with the dark hair and mustache is Rafe Cassidy. They rode for me once, 'til I got rid of 'em. Then they rode for first one rancher then another, 'til one by one ever'one got sick of 'em. I guess they been fired by ever' spread within fifty miles. Now they mostly drift about, rounding up a few strays for their money."

"Yeah, and sometimes the strays aren't even strayed yet," Doc said. "What gets me is why you ranchers don't know that."

"We know it," Louis admitted. "But we figure payin' a few bucks to get our strays back is better'n havin' 'em rustled."

"They're a rowdy bunch of bullies, all right," Doc said. "Don't nobody like 'em. In fact, I'm a little surprised to see them. They got drunk here two, maybe three weeks ago and tore up the place. Sheriff Grimes told them they was either goin' to have to pay for the damages or spend thirty days in jail."

"Which did they do?" Dane asked.

"Hell, they didn't do either one," Doc replied. "They just lit out. This is the first time they've been back since."

"I wonder if the sheriff knows they're in town," Ken said.

The three men who were the subject of the table conversation, perhaps sensing that they were being talked about, left the bar and wandered over to the card game.

"Well, now, this here looks like a friendly game,"

one of them said. This was Eli. "Any of you 'bout ready to give up your seats?"

No one answered.

"Hey, you, big guy," Eli said to Dane. Fred and Rafe laughed. "Why don't you take a rest for a while and let one of us sit in the game?"

"Hey, Eli, you want to play, you go right ahead," Fred said. "I didn't come into town to play no cards. Hell, we can do that out at the bunkhouse. I come for somethin' else."

"Yeah, Fred, we know what you come for," Rafe said. "You come to dip your wick."

The three men found that enormously funny.

"So, how 'bout it, big guy? You goin' to get up, or what?" Fred asked.

"I'm not ready to quit yet," Dane said.

"Is that so? Well, maybe if you'd win one big hand, you'd be ready," Eli suggested. "I'll help you." He started walking around the table. "Doc here has hisself a pair of jacks," he said. "Louis is holdin' a king, queen, and ace, but no pair." He stepped behind the leatherworker's chair. "Whooee. Now. Ken has two kings." He looked up. "Hope you can beat two kings."

Doc, Louis and Ken groaned, and Dane put his cards, down face up, on the table. He had two aces. "What do you say we leave the pot and re-deal?" he suggested to the others.

"Thanks. That's damned decent of you," Doc said.

"Hold it now, that's no way to be. I'm just trying to help." Eli smirked.

Dane glared at the ₊young cowboy. "I've had a

bellyful of you, mister," he said. "Back away from the table."

Dane's words were cold and clipped, and the easy banter fell away from the three young men. Eli licked his lips, the tip of his tongue darting out, snakelike.

"What did you say to me?"

"I told you to back away from the table."

"Mister, you don't think you can make words like that stick, do you?"

"I reckon I can."

"I don't know why I'm wastin' my time explainin' things to a dried-up bastard like you. Maybe I'm just an all-around nice guy. But someone ought to tell you that when you're sittin' down and I'm standin' up, there's no way you can get a gun out faster'n me. Now, you goin' to back up them words? Or you goin' to eat 'em?"

"I reckon I'll back 'em up," Dane said. During the entire confrontation one of his hands had been under the table. Now he brought it above the table and everyone gasped, because he was holding a Colt .44. Dane moved his lips into what could be called a smile, though the smile didn't quite reach the cold glint of his steel-blue eyes. "Looks like I did get it out faster, doesn't it? Now, you can try me, or you can go on about your business and leave us to ours."

The expression on the young cowboy's face changed from one of cockiness to fear. He put both hands up and started backing away.

"Listen, listen, mister," he said. "I didn't mean

nothin' by all this. I was just funnin', that's all. You boys go on now and enjoy your game."

"We intend to," Dane said.

The three cowboys walked away from the table.

Doc laughed. "Mister, if you won every hand for the rest of the night, it would be worth it," he said. "I've been wanting to see somebody stand up to those boys for a long time."

11

The three cowboys, after leaving the game table, returned to the bar for another drink. They were a bit more subdued than they had been when they first came in. Eli began drinking hard, tossing down one whiskey after another, while Fred and Rafe tried to calm him down. Finally Fred and Rafe gave up and left Eli to brood while they walked over to the table occupied by Smokey and Belle. Belle had stayed with Smokey, even though business had improved and it would have been much more profitable for her to leave him and begin working the crowd.

"Hello, Belle," Fred said.

Belle looked at him, then turned back to talk to Smokey.

"Hey Fred, what do you think? It looks like Belle don't love you no more," Rafe suggested.

"Yeah? Well, we'll see about that," Fred said. "Look here, you old fart," he said to Smokey. "If you ain't goin' to take Belle up to her room, then quit chewin' her ears off and let someone do it who's still young enough to get the job done."

Smokey turned in his chair and looked up at Fred. "You go ahead, sonny," he said. "Take her upstairs. I'll still be here when she's finished."

"Go ahead, Fred. You got his permission," Rafe teased.

"Yeah, well, I don't need the old goat's permission," Fred replied. He reached down to grab Belle's arm and she had to stand quickly to keep him from pulling her to her feet. "Tell you what, Rafe. Why don't you go back over there and have a drink with Eli? This here ain't goin' to take very long."

Smokey chuckled. "No," he said. "I don't reckon it will."

"What's that s'posed to mean?" Fred growled.

"Why, it don't mean nothin' at all, Fred," Smokey said. "I was just makin' conversation, that's all."

Fred laughed, a high-pitched laugh. "Yeah, well, seem's tha's 'bout all you're good for," he said. Tugging roughly on Belle's arm, he pulled her over to the stairs, then up to the second floor.

"I feel sorry for the girl," Ken said.

Doc looked up. "Yeah, well, don't worry about Belle. She's had plenty of experience handling people like that."

Though Dane said nothing, he tended to agree with Doc. He didn't like to see any woman, even a soiled dove, mistreated, but it had been his observation over the years that women like Belle were pretty good at protecting themselves.

Dane lost the re-dealt hand, then pushed himself away from the table. "I appreciate the game, gentlemen," he said. "But I think I'll just have a drink or two, then call it a night. Thanks for letting me sit in."

"We enjoyed your company, mister. New blood's always welcome, if it's friendly," Doc said. "What about it, Ken? Re-deal?"

"Not for me, thanks," Ken replied. "I think I'll call it a night, too."

"Me, too," Louis added. "We may as well break up the game now, or Eli will be over here again, wantin' to play."

"Yeah, I'll go along with that," Matt said.

"You fellas can quit if you want to, but I'd like to get the winning edge back," Doc said. "There are a couple of other games going on now. I think I'll see if I can join one of them."

Dane said goodbye to his friends, then walked over to the bar and ordered a drink. He had taken only one sip when the bat-wing doors swung open and a man wearing a badge, stepped into the saloon.

"It's Sheriff Grimes," someone said.

"Smoke's goin' to fly now, fellas," another put in. "He done give them three boys the word not to come back to town till they paid off the damages."

"Eli Stone," Sheriff Grimes called.

"Hello, Grimes. What got you away from your coffee and your nice, cushioned chair?"

"I smelled a stink in the air and I figured you was over here," Sheriff Grimes replied. "Did you bring one hundred dollars to cover the damages you caused the last time you was in town?"

"I told you I wasn't goin' to pay for them damages," Eli said without turning around.

"Then I reckon you'll be spendin' some time in jail."

Eli and Rafe both turned toward the sheriff. Eli smiled evilly at him.

"I don't reckon I'd care to do that, Grimes," Eli said. "You see, I'm pretty much what you'd call an outdoors man. Gettin' locked up in a jail ain't for me."

Sheriff Grimes held out his hand. "Give me your gun, Eli," he said. "You, too, Rafe."

Eli shook his head, the evil smile still pasted across his mouth.

"You want our guns, Sheriff, you're goin' to have to take 'em away from us. That is, if you think you're able to do it."

At Eli's challenging words, there was a sudden frenzied movement as people in the line of fire hurried to get out of the way. Only Eli and Rafe remained at the bar. Even Dane moved to the far end to be out of the way of any wild shot that might happen, should shooting break out.

"It doesn't have to be this way, boys," the sheriff said. "A few broken windows and chairs? It hardly seems worth dyin' over."

"That all depends on who's goin' to be dyin'," Eli said, moving his hand in position just over the handle of his pistol "You see, the way I'm figurin' is, you're the one that's goin' to do the dyin'."

Dane was a little surprised by Eli's bravado. He had already proven himself to be a braggart and a loudmouth, but when it came right down to it, braggarts and loudmouths usually caved in to calm courage. And this sheriff had already impressed Dane with the fact that he was a no-nonsense man of courage. What, then, was giving Eli his edge?

Dane sensed, more than saw or heard, the movement at the top of the stairs. When he looked up, he saw Fred, aiming at the sheriff. So, this was why Eli was so confident. He knew that Fred was upstairs with the drop on the sheriff, while the sheriff had no idea of the additional threat.

Ordinarily Dane never interfered in another man's fight. There were many reasons why he stayed out of them. Most of the time people resented interference, even if it had been undertaken with the best of intentions. Other times he just didn't know which side to back. This time, however, he had no problem with that. He had met the three cowboys and already disliked them enough to be partial to anyone who might be opposed to them. As it turned out, that was all the justification he needed to give the warning.

"Sheriff, there's a man on the landing with the drop on you," Dane warned loudly.

Angry that his ambush plans were spoiled by Dane's yell, Fred turned his gun on Dane.

"You ignorant fool!" he shouted, pulling the trigger even as he yelled.

Dane jumped to one side, pulling his pistol and shooting, almost as quickly as Fred. The slug that

Fred fired from the balcony missed Dane and slammed into the glass mirror behind the bar. The mirror shattered and fell, leaving only a few jagged shards hanging in place to reflect, in distorted images, the scene playing before it.

Fred didn't get away a second shot because Dane had fired right on top off him, and Dane's bullet found its mark. Fred dropped his pistol and grabbed his throat, then stood there, clutching his neck, as blood oozed between his fingers. Then his eyes rolled up into his head and he twisted and fell, sliding head-first down the stairs and following his clattering pistol all the way to the bottom. He lay motionless on the lowest step, his open but sightless eyes staring vacantly at the ceiling.

At the same time as Dane and Fred were having their shoot-out, Eli and the sheriff had also joined in the ball. Dane was still watching Fred slide down the stairs when he heard the roar of two more Colts. Though it seemed to him that time had stilled, thus causing a great separation between his and Fred's shots and the next two shots, the truth was that the battle between Eli and the sheriff had taken place almost simultaneously with his own fight.

Eli had fired at the sheriff first, but his shot was badly placed. All it did was put a hole in the sheriff's hat. The sheriff's shot hit Eli in the forehead and Eli slid down to the floor in the sitting position, his body held up by the bar, his hands lying on the floor to each side of him. Like Fred, Eli had been killed instantly.

"No, no, don't shoot! Don't shoot!" Rafe shouted,

holding his hands up in the air. "I ain't in this fight! I ain't in this fight!"

"Shuck your belt," the sheriff ordered.

"I'm doin' it, I'm doin' it," Rafe said, using his left hand to unfasten his belt buckle. The gun belt dropped to the floor with a clatter.

The sheriff looked at Rafe for a long moment, and Dane could almost believe he was going to shoot anyway. Finally he sighed and made a waving motion with his pistol.

"Get out of here, Rafe," the sheriff said. "Just thank goodness you got out of here alive. Leave town and don't ever come back."

"But Eli and Fred," Rafe said, taking in the two dead bodies with a sweep of his arm.

"We'll take care of the dead," the sheriff promised. "Now, if you don't want to wind up in jail for a very long time…get out of here."

"I'm goin', I'm goin'," Rafe said, starting for the door.

The sheriff looked toward Dane, then put his pistol away. Dane did the same.

"I owe you my thanks, mister," he said.

"Yeah, well, I didn't plan to get involved," Dane said. "But he didn't leave me much choice."

The sheriff looked at Dane, then up toward the top of the stairs where Fred had been standing, then back to Dane. "That's a pretty good shot, mister," he said. "You know, I'd make that better'n sixty feet. Would you agree?"

"That's as good a guess as any," Dane said.

"It's seventy-five feet if it's an inch," Doc insisted. He had gone over to Fred and was now examining the cowboy's wound. He didn't need to examine Eli. With a hole in his forehead, his eyes wide open and opaque, and in the sitting position, leaning back against the bar, Eli was very obviously dead. "Seventy-five feet," Doc added, "and the bullet caught old Fred-boy here right in the windpipe. Yes, sir, I'd say that was one hell of a shot."

The sheriff looked more closely at Dane. "Say, I know you, don't I?"

"I don't believe we've had the pleasure," Dane replied.

"You're right, we've never met in person," the sheriff agreed. He shook his finger slightly as he pointed it at Dane. "But there's no need for us to have met for me to know who you are. I've heard enough stories about you that I ought to have recognized you on sight. If your size wasn't enough, why, there was also the way you handled that pistol. No, sir, you can't be no one else but that famous bounty hunter. Am I right?"

"I prefer to be called Dane."

Sheriff Grimes snapped his fingers and smiled broadly. "I'm right, aren't I? I knew I was right." He looked at the two bodies, which had now been picked up and laid out, side by side, on one of the longer tables. "Is there paper out on these boys? If so, I wasn't aware of it."

"I wasn't after them," Dane replied. "They just happened to get in the way."

"Who are you after?"

"I think I can tell you that," Doc volunteered.

"Oh? And who would that be?" the sheriff asked.

"Unless I miss my guess, he's after Charley Redford," Louis suggested to the sheriff. Then he looked directly at Dane. "That was pretty slick of you, Dane, to get into a card game with us just so you could get information," he added.

"I've learned that sometimes it's better to take the long way around," Dane explained.

"I guess that's right most of the time," Louis replied. "But the truth is, there isn't a man here who doesn't want to see Charley Redford and that bunch get their due. In case you missed what we were saying a while ago, a fire down Snake Canyon this time of year is awfully curious."

Grimes chuckled. "Louis, do you know you're givin' away information there that's worth fifteen hundred dollars?"

"Fifteen hundred dollars? How do you figure?" Louis asked.

"There's five hundred dollars' reward money out on Charley Redford, Hawk Doyle, and Clay Morrow," he said.

"Not Clay Morrow," Dane interjected.

"Yeah, him, too," the sheriff insisted. "He's worth as much as either one of the other two fellas."

"I've already collected on Morrow," Dane said matter-of-factly.

"When did you get him? The word we got was

there was three men held up the bank over in Santo Valle yesterday."

"That was Redford, Doyle, and Babbit. Nathan Babbit," Dane said. "Babbit is one of the two men who helped the three escape."

"What about the other man who helped them?" the sheriff asked. "Who is he?"

"Silas McGrath," Dane replied easily.

"Silas McGrath," the sheriff repeated. He shook his head. "You know, I don't recall even seein' a poster on that gentleman. If he comes through here, I won't even know him."

"Don't worry about him," Dane said easily.

"Well, I'd at least like to know if he—" The sheriff stopped in midsentence. "You got him, too, didn't you?"

"Yesterday afternoon."

"You're a busy man, Mr. Calder."

"I try to do my job, Sheriff Grimes."

"Who is this Nathan Babbit, Grimes?" Doc asked. "Have you ever heard of him?"

"Yes, I've heard of him," Grimes answered. "He's a mean one, all right. Maybe even meaner than the others."

"As far as I'm concerned, any money Dane Calder gets from handling people like Redford and Babbit and the others, he's entitled to. Believe me, I have no interest in trying to collect any of it for myself." Louis looked at Dane. "So if the knowledge that Redford and his bunch may be poking around down in Snake

Canyon is useful to you, have it, and have it with my blessing."

"Thanks," Dane said. "I reckon I'll be checking that place out."

DANE'S WEREN'T the only ears to hear the possible location of Charley Redford. Rafe Cassidy had been run out of the saloon a few minutes earlier by the sheriff, but he hadn't actually gone anywhere. Right now he was standing in the shadows by the bat-wing doors just outside the saloon. With his back to the wall and a small, two-shot sleeve gun cradled in his raised, right hand, Rafe planned to shoot Dane the moment he stepped outside.

As he listened, however, he began to have other plans. If Redford and his gang were worth that much money to Dane Calder...how much money would Calder be worth to them?

Ned Wells wasn't the only one who had seen the campfire last night. Rafe, Fred, and Eli had seen it too. And not only did Rafe know where it was, he knew a shorter way to get there. If he could get to Charley Redford and his gang before Calder and provide them with information as to when and where Dane Calder would come for them, they would be mighty grateful. They might even let him join them.

12

Rafe was pretty deep into the canyon at the mouth of McKenzie Draw. Though there were literally dozens of draws and gullies in the canyon that would offer shelter, McKenzie Draw was the only one that offered a way back out. When Rafe stopped just outside the mouth of the draw, he climbed up onto a protruding finger and looked over into it.

It was too dark to see anything, so he decided to wait until dawn. There were three of them and only one of him, and he had no desire to stumble into their camp in the middle of the night. That would be a good way to get himself killed.

When Rafe looked to the east, he could see a faint streak of pearl gray. It wouldn't be much longer until it was light enough for him to approach. He could afford to wait it out. If they would listen to him, and believe him, they would still have time to prepare an ambush for Calder.

Rafe pulled a strip of jerky from his saddlebag,

chewed off a piece, then wrapped what remained in the soiled and greasy waxed paper he kept it in. He chewed it for several minutes and it seemed to get bigger and bigger in his mouth. He wanted to spit it out, but he figured he would need the sustenance, so he continued to work at it. He finally managed to get the last bit down, then he followed that with a swallow of water. He wished it was coffee, but he knew that starting a fire would be foolish...perhaps even fatal.

The night finally lifted, illuminating the canyon floor in a soft, coral light, though lingering shadows still hung in the corners and edges of the deeper draws. Rafe climbed up to the top of the protruding finger and looked down into McKenzie Draw once more. This time he saw the camp, but he was surprised to see that there was only one person there. He knew there were at least three of them. Where were the other two?

"Oh, you clever bastards," he said quietly. "You're keeping two men on watch while one sleeps. That way nobody can sneak in on you."

He wondered, though, why they had not yet come in. He also wondered why the lone man in camp had not built a fire for their morning coffee. Maybe they were being cautious. Why weren't they that cautious the other night? Every nighthawk within twenty miles had seen the fire then.

Rafe chuckled to himself as he thought of an old saying. He said it aloud. "You boys have done shut the barn door after the horse is gone," he said.

Rafe stood up, brushed his hands together, then started walking down the other side of the little hill into the campsite.

"Hello the camp!" he called, holding his arms out so that anyone watching could clearly see that he wasn't carrying a weapon. "Hello the camp! I'm a friend!"

The two lookouts didn't come in, nor did they even make their presence known.

"Mr. Redford?" Rafe called. "Charley Redford? My name is Rafe Cassidy. I've come to join you, if I may."

Still no answer or movement. Even the one person in the camp was still.

"Listen, I want to warn you. That big bounty hunter is on his way out here. Someone give him some information that you were out here. It wasn't me," he added. "I swear, it wasn't me. I just overheard which is how come I'm here."

Rafe was beginning to get a little disconcerted. Neither of the two lookouts had given any indication as to their presence, and even the lone man in the camp was quiet.

"Mister, are you asleep? You can't be asleep. Hell, I've made more noise than a herd of cows comin' into this camp." By now Rafe was right over the supine figure, and he squatted down to touch him on the shoulder. "What's the matter with you?"

The man on the ground suddenly rolled over. Rafe saw a flash of movement, then felt the barrel of the man's pistol under his chin. He heard the hammer being cocked.

"Who are you?" the man asked.

"Rafe Cassidy. Rafe Cassidy," Rafe said in fright, backing away so quickly that he fell on his back. "Don't shoot! Don't shoot!"

The man sat up, though it seemed to be with some effort. He held his gun leveled toward Rafe. "What are you doing here?" he asked.

"I came to warn you and the others about Calder. You know that big bounty hunter."

The man with the gun laughed, then he winced with pain and put his hand down to his hip. That was when Rafe saw that his right pants leg was caked with dried blood.

"You're hurt?" he asked.

"Yeah. Some kid shot me with a twenty-two." He laughed again, a dry brittle laugh. "Can you believe that? Hawk Doyle gettin' shot by a kid? With a twenty-two?"

"You're Hawk Doyle?"

"Yeah, that's me." Doyle squinted at Rafe. "Who'd you say you was again?"

"My name is Rafe, Mr. Doyle. Rafe Cassidy."

"What are you doin' out here, Rafe?"

"Like I told you, I come to warn you about Dane Calder."

"Why would you do that?"

"Well, for one thing, I don't like him very much," Rafe said. "He killed one of my friends yesterday. And for another, I thought maybe you and Mr. Redford and Mr. Babbit would let me join up with you."

Doyle laughed again, another dry, brittle, laugh.

"You want to ride the outlaw trail do you, Rafe?" he asked.

"Yes."

"You're bold and brave and you want to join that gallant band of brothers whose home is the wind and whose destiny is danger?"

"What?"

Doyle laughed heartily. "I got that from one of those dime novels some fool wrote about Charley. Charley carries them with him, you know, and if he finds somebody who hasn't heard of him, he shows them the books."

"I never knew they wrote no books about Charley Redford."

"You've never heard of Cactus Charley?"

"I've heard of Charley Redford," Rafe said. "I never heard him called Cactus Charley."

Doyle laughed again. "Charley won't like that," he said. "He sets a great store by those dime novels."

Rafe looked around nervously.

"Where is he?" he asked. "I thought there was three of you. Are the others standing watch?"

"Yeah, they're standing watch," Doyle said. "By now they're watching the whores dance in Loma Alta."

"Loma Alta? That's a hundred miles south of here, near to the border."

"That's the general idea," Doyle replied.

"But what are you doin' here?" Rafe looked around the campsite. "Where's your horse?"

"You noticed that, did you? My horse is gone. They

took it with them...along with my share of the money from the bank in Santo Valle, and my water and my food. If the bastards could've turned me in for the five-hundred-dollar reward money, they would've done that, too. You got any water?"

"Yeah. My canteen's on the horse. Why did they leave you here like this?"

"They thought I'd slow 'em down," Doyle said. "Get me some water, will you?"

"Sure," Rafe said. He went back for his horse, and as he was loosening the hobble, he saw a plume of dust in the distance, glowing brightly in the early morning sun. He hurried his horse back into the camp. "Someone's coming," he said.

"Calder?"

"It has to be," Rafe replied. He handed his canteen to Doyle, who, thirstily, took several long swallows. "Easy, it's ten miles to the nearest water hole."

Doyle handed the canteen back to Rafe. "Thanks," he said.

"What are we goin' to do about Calder?" Rafe asked.

"You got a rifle?"

"Yeah, I got a rifle."

"Tell you what you do. You tie your horse here, then you take your rifle and go over there, in those rocks, and wait. I'll be the bait, you see. And when Calder comes into the camp, you'll have a perfect bead on him."

"Yeah," Rafe said. "Yeah, that's a good idea."

"Leave me your pistol."

"What do you want with my pistol?"

"That's a thirty-seven, isn't it?"

"Yes."

"Mine's a forty-four. I don't have no bullets and what you got won't fit mine."

"You don't have any shells at all?"

"None," Hawk replied. He thought of the empty metal click last night when, in despair, he had put the pistol to his temple and pulled the trigger. "I reckon Charley and Nathan thought I wouldn't have no need for 'em out here. When they left, they took everything, even the shells that was already loaded into my gun."

"No bullets at all, huh?" Rafe smiled when he got the idea. "Well, I'll be damned."

DANE STOPPED when he heard the shot, flat and low in the distance. If he had been closer, he might have thought someone was shooting at him, but it was much too far to do that. Why would they be shooting? Didn't they realize that in so doing, they were giving away their position? Dane reached down to pat the neck of his animal.

"Could be that they know I'm here and they're just lettin' me know they know," Dane suggested to his horse. His horse, almost as if understanding, whickered. Dane chuckled. "That's what you think, too, huh? Well, come on, let's see this thing through."

As Dane moved up the canyon floor, he

approached carefully by staying close to the wall, taking advantage of the many rocks and protrusions, passing through apertures when possible rather than going around or over the long fingers. When he reached one particularly large protrusion, he saw horse droppings that were just a few hours old. He saw, too, that there were more horse droppings than would be there from the casual passing of an animal. The horse that did this had lingered in this very spot for quite a while.

Dane moved cautiously up to the top of the promontory, then looked over to the other side. He saw a hobbled, saddled horse and Hawk Doyle sitting nearby, holding a coffee cup and staring into the remains of a fire.

There was something not quite right about the scene, and Dane studied it for a long moment trying to figure out what was wrong. Gradually it began to come to him.

The first thing peculiar was the stillness with which Doyle was sitting there. Dane had been watching him for almost a full minute now, and Doyle had not only not taken a drink of his coffee, he hadn't even moved or twitched. Besides, Dane wondered if he did have coffee in that cup, where did it come from? There was no pot anywhere, no smell of coffee in the air, and not even a tiny wisp of smoke to indicate that the coals were still warm.

Dane realized then, as much from gut instinct as from what he was seeing that Doyle was dead. That was what the shot was. They said that the kid who was killed in Santo Valle had hit one of the robbers. Dane knew now what happened. Hawk Doyle was the one who was hit, and because he was slowing them down, the other two had killed him and left him behind as a decoy.

With a sigh, Dane holstered his pistol and started down into the camp. The carcass was still worth five hundred dollars to him, so there was no way he was going to leave him here. Conveniently Doyle's horse was still here, too, so all Dane would have to do would be throw him belly-down on the saddle and...the saddle?

Suddenly Dane realized that something else was wrong! There was one saddle too many! One was on the ground beside the propped-up body of Hawk Doyle, and the other was on the horse.

At that moment a rifle cracked and the bullet whistled by, taking off his hat and fluffing his hair. Dane dived to the ground, pulling his pistol from his holster as he did so. He began wriggling on his belly toward a small rock outcropping, reaching it just as a second bullet came so close that he could hear the air pop as it sped by.

When he made it to the rocks, he raised up and slowly looked toward the source of the shot. He didn't see anyone, but he did see a little puff of white smoke drifting slowly to the east. Because the wind was out of the west, that meant that the shooter had to be somewhat west of the smoke. Dane shifted his eyes in that direction then saw the crown of a hat, rising slowly above the rocks.

Dane waited until he thought enough of the hat was visible to provide a target, then he shot. The hat went sailing away.

"Hey, Mister, you put a hole in my hat!"

"I meant to put a hole in your head," Dane replied. He was puzzled by the voice. This wasn't Charley Redford or Nathan Babbit. Who was it?

The ambusher fired again. The bullet hit the rock right in front of Dane, kicking up tiny pieces of rock and shreds of hot lead to his face before it whined away behind him. Dane turned around and slid down into the ground, brushing the hot lead from his cheeks.

"Did I mess up your pretty face?" the man called out.

"Close, but no cigar," Dane replied. "Who the hell are you?"

The man laughed. "You don't recognize me?" he asked. "All I can say is, you sure got yourself one hell of a short memory."

Dane remembered now…not the name, but the voice. "You were in the saloon last night," he said. "You were with the two who got themselves killed."

"Yeah. The name's Rafe Cassidy, in case you forgot."

"Rafe Cassidy," Dane said. "I'll try to remember that."

"You won't have to remember it too long," He fired again—again coming incredibly close.

Dane realized then that Rafe Cassidy wasn't just

another wild cowboy with a gun. He was very good with the rifle.

"I'll say this for you, Rafe Cassidy. You handle that rifle pretty well."

"Yeah," Rafe said. "There wasn't no way I was goin' to go up against you or the sheriff with a pistol last night. But with a rifle, now, that's a different story. I've won the Fourth-of-July rifle-shooting contest for the last five years running."

"That's pretty good," Dane said.

"Yeah," Rafe replied. "Good enough, I figure, to do me in good stead for my new business."

"Let me guess, Rafe. Would that be the bounty-hunting business?"

"You guessed right," Rafe replied. "I come out here to join up with 'em, only I found Doyle here, all alone. The others had gone on to Loma Alta without him. Me and Doyle got to talkin' and the next thing you know, I find out he's worth five hundred dollars. He wasn't lyin' to me, was he Calder? He is worth five hundred dollars?"

"He wasn't lyin', He's worth that and then some," Dane answered, thinking of the additional reward Judge Sweeny had put on his head.

"Yeah, well five hundred dollars. That's a lot of money," Rafe said. "So I got to thinkin' about it. Why should I join up with these fellas and get a price on my head when I could turn him in and get the reward myself? So I killed him."

"Seems like the reasonable thing to do," Dane said.

During the entire conversation, Dane had been slipping out of his boots, pants, and shirt. Now he put them on the ground behind where he had taken cover, arranging them so that, at a casual glance from a distance, it would look as if he were there. Then, barefoot and half-naked, he put the blade of his knife between his teeth and slipped away. After having gone some thirty yards, he found himself in a narrow, twisting fissure that worked its way down the side of the canyon, passing fairly close to where Rafe had taken cover.

Dane stepped into the fissure and, putting his bare feet and hands on either side, began climbing. Not even a mountain goat would be able to climb up this steep, natural chimney, but Dane wasn't a mountain goat. He was a man who had lived with the Apache…a people who could climb where mountain goats could not.

"I figure the first thing I got to do if I'm goin' to be a success at my new business is get rid of my competition," Rafe said. He chuckled. "That's you, Calder."

Rafe fired again and his bullet nicked the heel of Dane's boot, knocking it back behind the rock.

"Ha!" Rafe shouted. "I'll just reckon that stung a mite, didn't it? That'll learn you to keep your foot out where I can see it."

Dane continued to climb until he reached a ledge. Once there, he left the fissure and crawled out onto it. Then, on his stomach, he wriggled over to the edge and looked down. Rafe was no more than twenty yards below him. Rafe was peering around the side of a rock, looking toward the place where he had last seen Dane.

"Hey, Calder! How come you ain't shootin' back?" Rafe called. "You ain't out of shells, are you? 'Course, if you was, I don't reckon you'd tell me. I mean, Hawk Doyle told me an' look what it got him. Like you said, it seemed like the reasonable thing to do."

Rafe fired again.

"If you keep shooting at rocks, you're going to run out of bullets yourself," Dane said easily.

Startled, Rafe turned around. The expression on his face reflected the shock of seeing Dane, not only in a place totally different from where he thought he was, but also because Dane was naked, except for a pair of underbriefs.

"What the hell?" Rafe shouted, swinging his rifle around while, at the same time, jacking in a new round.

Rafe got the lever down, but he never pulled it back up. Dane's right arm whipped forward and the knife flashed once in the sun as it sped across the distance between the two men. It buried itself to the hilt in Rafe's chest, penetrating his heart and killing him even before he could fully realize what was happening to him.

13

L oma Alta was on the American side of the border, but far more Mexicans lived there than Americans. Its primary reason for being was to provide a conduit between Mexico and the United States. Mexican peasants who were leaving their homeland for a better life stopped here on their way north. Americans, many of whom were going to Mexico to escape wanted posters, stopped here on their way south.

The land immediately around Loma Alta was arid and too poor for farming or ranching. Many tried, though, and a few even managed to eke out a meager existence. There were some who searched for gold or silver, and though little of those commodities were found, enough nuggets turned up to hold out tantalizing prospects. Thus the hunt continued.

Despite the bleakness of its agricultural and mining industries, Loma Alta was a bustling town. It saw a surprising amount of money flow through its

half-dozen saloons, whorehouses, gaming establish-
ments, cafés, and hotels. Outlaws fleeing south often
used Loma Alta for one last American fling. And since
many of those same outlaws were fleeing from bank
robberies or other sources of ill-gotten gain, money
was in abundance. On the other hand, Mexicans just
arriving in America would often spend their life
savings in one afternoon, too ignorant of the
exchange system to know they were being cheated.

Loma Alta had a sheriff and two deputies. One
wall in the sheriff's office was decorated with wanted
posters from both sides of the border. However,
neither Sheriff Woodridge nor his deputies had ever
made any attempt to apprehend the men on the
wanted posters. The way the sheriff explained it, he
and his deputies were hired by the people in Loma
Alta to keep the peace in Loma Alta. If a man who had
a price on his head in Texas, or Colorado, or
Wyoming, or some such place happened to pass
through Loma Alta, he was just as welcome as any
other traveler, so long as he didn't disturb the peace in
Loma Alta.

The outlaws were very aware of Sheriff
Woodridge's policy toward wanted men, so they were
always on their best behavior in his town and around
him. In fact, some of them even became friends with
him and the sheriff's "rogues' gallery" became somewhat well known throughout the southwest for a
most unique reason. Almost three-quarters of the
wanted posters on the wall in his office were auto-
graphed by the very outlaws whose face graced them.

Babbit was very familiar with Loma Alta, having been there many times before. However, it was Charley's first visit, so Babbit explained the ground rules to him as they rode toward the town.

"All you gotta do when we get there is keep your nose clean here," Babbit told him. "Don't get in any fights."

"If nobody messes with me, there won't be no problem," Charley replied.

"No fights, Charley," Babbit repeated. "If somebody messes with you, you're goin' to let them. You understand what I'm saying?"

"This is my gang, Nathan. I give the orders, not you," Charley replied.

Babbit laughed. "Look around, Charley. You been gettin' shed of your gang like a dog scratchin' off fleas. You see anyone left?"

"All right, all right," Charley said. "I'll stay outta trouble."

"That's a good boy, Charley."

"But I ain't your boy," Charley said, holding up his finger to make his point. "And soon as I can, I'm puttin' together another gang."

"Yeah, Charley, you do that."

"How much longer?" Charley asked. "I'm gettin' hungry for somethin' more'n jerky and thirsty for more'n trail water."

"Couple hours, maybe," Babbit replied. "We'll be there by nightfall."

TRUE TO BABBIT'S ESTIMATE, it was just after dark when he and Charley rode into town, butt weary from the long ride down. They had seventy-five dollars apiece from the bank job in Santo Valle. In most towns, seventy-five dollars would be considered a lot of money, but Babbit was quick to point out that it wouldn't go far here.

"A whore's two dollars anywhere else," he explained. "Here, they're five dollars."

"Mexican or American?" Charley wanted to know.

"Both, I reckon."

Loma Alta was dark except for the patches of light that spilled out into the street from the windows and doors of the cantinas. The town was noisy...several guitars competed with each other for attention, a few people were singing, and in the back of one of the cantinas, a trumpet ran through several high trills. Laughter and loud voices filled the night air, and occasionally a gunshot would ring out, though the people knew, almost instinctively, that the gunshots were in boisterous fun and nothing more.

"Hey, fellas," a woman called down to them from an upstairs balcony as they rode by. She was leaning over a banister, wearing nothing but an undergarment that was cut low enough to expose the tops of enormous breasts. Her breasts were large because she was large. "Hey, fellas, why don't both of you come on up here?" she invited. "I'll take both of you on for the price of one."

With her red hair, pasty-white complexion, and flat, twangy accent, she was definitely American.

"You want to give her a try?" Babbit asked.

Charley looked up at the woman, then laughed. "No, I don't think so," he said. "I'd rather find me a dark-eyed Mexican woman."

"What do you say we get us somethin' to drink?"

The drinking establishment was much more Mexican in flavor than American and even had a clacking curtain of beaded strings for its entry rather than the more American bat-wing doors. Inside, the bar was noisy with conversation, half of it in Spanish, half of it in English.

"Hello, señor," a pretty, young Mexican girl said, coming up to Charley. "I am very thirsty and I do not want to drink alone. You will drink with me?"

Charley started to reach for her, then he saw the top of her full, creamy breasts, spilling out over her low-cut blouse.

"No," he said. "Go find someone else."

"What the hell's the matter with you, Charley?" Babbit asked, surprised by Charley's strange reaction. "I thought you said you wanted some good-lookin' Mexican gal."

"No...not now," Charley said.

"Well if you don't want her, I do," Babbit said. He put his arm around the girl. "Come on, honey. You want a drink, let's get a whole bottle and go upstairs."

Of the two men, Babbit was clearly the less attractive to the woman. In fact, there was something almost frightening about his yellow eyes and that terrible scar on his face. That was why she had made her initial overture to Charley. But he had refused, and in her business, she couldn't afford to be choosy. So she kept the disappointment hidden behind her eyes and pasted on a smile.

"All right," she said to Babbit. "If your friend does not want me, then I will go with you." Teasingly, she put her hand in Babbit's hair and twisted a strand of it around her finger. "If you want me," she added coquettishly.

"Honey, you come with me and I'll show you just how much I want you," Babbit said, grabbing her and walking over to the bar to buy a bottle.

Charley watched Babbit and the Mexican girl take their bottle up the stairs, then he, too, walked over to the bar.

"Can I get anything to eat here?" he asked.

"Frijoles. Tamales," the bartender answered.

"Anything American?"

"Eggs, señor."

"Steak?"

The bartender nodded. "Si, steak, too."

"Fix me a steak and some eggs," Charley said. "And let me have a pitcher of beer."

"Si, Señor Charley. Anything you want," the bartender replied.

Charley smiled. "You know who I am? You recognize me?"

"No, señor. But Señor Babbit called you Charley. Is that not your name, señor?"

The smile left Charley's face. "Yeah," he said, somewhat crestfallen. "Yeah, that's my name."

14

C harley took the pitcher of beer from the bartender and walked over to an empty table in the corner. He sat down with his back to the wall and began drinking his beer. Then he reached into his back pocket and pulled out a rolled-up dime novel and laid it on the table to admire. The pages were torn and the printing was getting dim from sweat, grime, and wear. The drawing on the cover was still discernible, however, and Charley studied it for a long time. It showed a man on a horse, fleeing before a posse. Hanging across the pommel of his saddle were two large bags, and if the reader couldn't figure out what the bags were, they were clearly marked by oversized dollar signs.

In the background was a train. The door of the mail car was open and someone was standing in the opening, holding his fist over his head. A word balloon from the mouth of the character said: *Cactus Charley! He has just robbed the express!*

There were several people leaning out the open windows of the cars on the train and all of them seemed to be armed and shooting at the fleeing robber. The robber, who according to the book, was Cactus Charley Redford, was holding the reins of his horse in his teeth while he was twisted around in the saddle, firing both guns at the pursuing posse, two of whom were in the process of falling from their saddles with mortal wounds, inflicted by Cactus Charley's unerring pistol fire.

The cover left unexplained how a posse managed to arrive on the scene so quickly that the train Cactus Charley had just robbed was still sitting on the tracks. It also did not take into account the fact that of all the crimes for which the real Charley Redford was charged, none of them involved robbing a train, which was, in fact, much too dangerous an operation for Charley ever to consider.

The name of the novel was *Cactus Charley's Bold Midnight Robbery of the Denver Express,* though the robbery depicted on the cover was very obviously taking place in daylight.

Charley began to read:

He came upon the train with both guns blazing and the reins of his horse held in his teeth. "Stand and deliver!" he shouted in a voice that was both heroic and frightening.

Charley thought this was a very exciting beginning. He never stopped to wonder how he could even talk with the reins in his teeth, let alone sound off in a voice that was both heroic and frightening. And though he had never used the line *stand and deliver,* it had a good ring to it and he decided that in his next holdup he would use it.

"It is Cactus Charley," the engineer shouted to his fireman. His voice was laced with fear and respect, for Cactus Charley is known throughout the West as the deadliest shot alive. It has been reliably reported that Cactus Charley can shoot the leg off a fly at fifty paces. There was a shower of sparks and the squeal of steel wheels sliding upon steel rails as the frightened engineer brought his great iron steed to rest.

"Open the doors of the express car or feel the fury of hot lead!" Cactus Charley demanded.

Though the armed guards of the express car were filled with the greatest of trepidation, the ladies of the train, all of whom had hurried to the windows as a more opportune place from which to get a good look, were strangely devoid of fear. They seemed, instead, romantically smitten by the handsome young man who sat astride his horse, holding the brace of pistols leveled at the express car door.

A PLATE of steak and eggs was put on the table in front of Charley, but he was too absorbed in the story to bother to look up. He reached for the steak and picked it up in his hands.

"Charley, you really need to work on your table manners," Dane said. "Haven't you ever heard of a knife and fork?"

Gasping, Charley looked up to see that the person who had just delivered his food was not the bartender but Dane Calder. Dane had his pistol out. He waved the end of the barrel.

"Go ahead, take a bite," he said. "I wouldn't want to disturb a man before he was finished eatin' his supper."

Charley held the piece of meat just in front of his mouth, staring wide-eyed at this captor.

"Go ahead, eat," Dane said again.

Charley raised the steak to his mouth, then suddenly dropped it and make a mad grab for his pistol. But Dane was quicker and he brought his pistol down hard on Charley's head. Charley fell like a pole-axed steer.

"You shouldn't read that trash, Charley," Dane said quietly. "You'll get to believing you're better than you are."

Dane bent down to take Charley's pistol. Then he dragged the outlaw's limp, unconscious form over to one of the supporting posts where he propped him and, placing one arm to either side of the post, put the handcuffs on.

The guitar music, laugher, and conversation had all come to a stop when Dane knocked Charley out. Most of the other patrons looked on in curiosity, making no comment until they saw Dane put on the handcuffs.

"Hey, what the hell? You a lawman, mister? 'Cause if you are, you got no jurisdiction here."

Dane looked up at the speaker. "Who are you?" he asked.

"I'm the man that's goin' to teach you better'n to

come into Loma Alta to serve paper. Who the hell are you?"

"The name is Calder, Dane Calder."

"Calder?" someone said in a high, choked voice.

"That there is the bounty hunter," another added in a harsh whisper.

"*El cazarrecompensas*," one of the Mexicans said in awe.

The man who had challenged Dane began to shake. "Don't pay me no mind, mister," he said in a frightened, quavering voice. "You go on about your business."

"Obliged," Dane replied. He walked back over to the table where Charley had been sitting. His untouched steak had fallen back onto his plate and Dane cut off a generous piece of it and stuck it into his mouth. He picked up the pitcher of beer and took several swallows before he sat it back down. The rest of the saloon continued to watch him in silence.

"Play," Dane said to the guitarist.

"Si, señor," the guitarist said, and he began strumming some chords.

Dane walked over to the bar. "There were two of 'em," he said.

"Si, señor."

"Where's the other one?"

"Señor, I cannot say," the bartender replied. "Please, do not ask me." Even as he was refusing to speak, however, he flicked his eyes up.

"All right," Dane replied. "I'll find him myself."

Upstairs, in the girl's bedroom, Babbit had heard the saloon below grow strangely quiet. He stopped.

"Are you finished, señor?" the girl asked.

"Shut up," Babbit hissed.

"*Que?*" the girl asked, surprised by Babbit's harsh words.

"I said shut up!" Babbit said again, putting his hand over her mouth. When he was sure she wouldn't speak again, he pulled his hand away. The girl took a long, gasping breath.

Babbit sat up and swung his legs over the side of the bed, then reached for his pistol. It was still deathly quiet below. "Don't you hear that?" he asked.

"I hear nothing, señor," the girl said in a quiet, whimpering voice.

"Yeah, that's just it," Babbit said. "Neither do I."

Still holding his pistol, he began slipping back into his pants. He was already buttoning them up when the guitar music started again. Even this, however, was different. Before, the music had been soft and melodious, a simple melody weaving in and out of gentle chording. Now it was loud, syncopated, and invasive.

Babbit slipped into his boots and kept his eye on the doorknob. He had just gotten them on when he saw the doorknob move ever so slightly.

Babbit began firing, punching a pattern of six bullets through the door in such a way that one of them was sure to be fatal to whoever was on the other side.

With an angry shout, Babbit rushed across the room and kicked open the door. He ran out onto the landing just outside the door.

Dane had jiggled the doorknob then stepped to one side, no more than a second before the fusillade of bullets. He stood on one side of the door with his back to the wall, watching the spray of splinters as the bullets came through. Then he heard Babbit's loud, angry shout as the outlaw dashed across the room. When the fugitive appeared on the landing, Dane brought his pistol crashing into the back of his head. The blow, plus the momentum of Babbit's rush carried him through the banister, causing him to crash, belly-down, onto one of the tables in the room below.

By the time Dane reached the bottom of the stairs, Sheriff Woodridge was stepping through the beaded curtains of the front door. He saw all the patrons of the saloon standing to one side or the other, giving Dane a lot of room.

"What the hell is goin' on here?" the sheriff asked.

"I have a couple of prisoners for you, Sheriff," Dane said. He pointed to Charley. "The one handcuffed to the post is Charley Redford. The other one is Nathan Babbit."

The sheriff shook his head. "I got no call to hold them two fellas," he said. "They ain't done nothin' in my town."

"All I want you to do is keep them overnight while

I get a little sleep." Dane reached into his shirt pocket and took out two folded papers. "They're both wanted men," he said. "Here are the dodgers. All I want you to do is keep them overnight. I'll be takin' 'em back with me in the morning."

"They may be wanted men where you come from, mister," the sheriff said. "But like I said, they ain't wanted here. I'm not puttin' 'em in my jail."

By now Charley had come to and heard the sheriff's refusal to cooperate.

"What are you goin' to do now, Calder?" he asked. "You got to have some rest 'fore you start back. Otherwise you might just drop off to sleep and me or Babbit will get the jump on you." He giggled loudly at his suggestion.

"Don't worry about it, Charley," Dane said. "The sheriff has just changed his mind. He's going to keep you two for me after all."

"Now, just a minute here!" Sheriff Woodridge said. "Where do you come off sayin' a thing like that? I ain't about to change my mind."

Dane's draw was as quick as the flick of a rattler's tongue. He raised his pistol and pointed it at Sheriff Woodridge. "Sheriff, you can go down to the jailhouse as their jailer or their cellmate. The choice is yours."

"Suppose I don't like either choice?" the sheriff replied.

"There is a third choice," Dane explained. "You can go out of here stretched out flat on your back." He cocked his pistol.

"I'm the sheriff. You wouldn't shoot me."

Dane fired. His bullet clipped off a tiny piece of the sheriff's left earlobe, sending out a spray of blood. The sheriff, with a shout of pain and terror, slapped his hand to his ear. The wound was bleeding profusely and the blood began streaming through his fingers.

"You're...you're crazy!" he said.

Dane moved the pistol to aim at the sheriff's other ear. Quickly Woodridge covered it up.

"This time I'll take off a couple of fingers, too," Dane suggested.

"No! No! Wait!" the sheriff said, holding his bloody hands, palms out, toward Dane. "Don't shoot again. I'll put 'em up for you!"

Dane smiled and lowered his gun. "I thank you for your cooperation," he said. "Come first light in the mornin', I'll be by for them."

15

A crowing rooster woke Dane just before first light the next morning. He sat up, stretched, pulled on his boots, then walked over to the dry sink, where he poured water from a pitcher into a basin and splashed a little onto his face. A few minutes later he tromped downstairs, past the snoring hotel clerk, and out into the early-morning coolness.

Loma Alta in the morning and Loma Alta in the evening were like two different towns. Last night the streets had been noisy with high-pitched laughter, boisterous song, loud talk, and banging guns, some discharged in fun, some in anger. But even the most dedicated reveler was in bed now, and the only sounds to be heard were the sounds of the other half of the town…the working half…coming awake.

A freight wagon was being loaded, and Dane could hear the scrape, roll, and drop of its cargo being put into place.

A woman was doing her wash, and Dane could

hear the scruffing sounds of wet clothes being rubbed back and forth across a washboard.

Another early riser was doing some carpentry work and Dane could hear the rip and tear of the saw teeth, chewing into the piece of lumber.

Dane woke the stable boy and paid the fare for his horse and for Charley and Babbit's horses. The animals looked fit and ready for the trip back to Coyote Springs. That was good, since he had no desire to have his trip interrupted by problems with one of the mounts.

Dane rode his horse and led the other two down to the far end of the street. It was curious, he thought, how three horses could walk down a main street at high noon and barely be heard. This morning, however, the fall of their hooves seemed so loud that he doubted if he could have made any more noise had he been banging on a drum. He stopped in front of the sheriff's office and tied up at the hitching rail.

The sheriff was already up this morning, sitting at his desk. He had a bandage covering his shot-up ear; it was wound all the way around his head. As a result he looked much more seriously hurt than he was. He was drinking coffee and eating a biscuit and he glared at Dane when Dane came into the office.

"Good morning, Sheriff," Dane said. "Good, you fixed breakfast."

"Not for you, I didn't," the sheriff growled.

Dane walked over to the stove and hefted the coffeepot, then he opened the saver and looked in to see a pan full of biscuits.

"That's for my deputies," the sheriff said.

Dane clinked a half-dollar down on the corner of the sheriff's desk. "Tell 'em to get their breakfast somewhere else," he ordered. He filled two cups, then grabbed four biscuits and started back to the cells. "Charley, Babbit, wake up," he called. "It's time to be goin'." He passed the coffee and biscuits through the bars.

"You poison this?" Charley asked.

"Now, why would I poison you, Charley?" Dane answered good-naturedly. "If I didn't want to see you hang, I would've shot you last night. Besides, seeing as how you missed your supper, I figured you might be hungry this morning."

Babbit took his breakfast without comment, and the two men returned to their bunk where they sat down to eat.

"Don't get to thinking you're having breakfast at Delmonico's," Dane told them. "Swallow that down pretty quick. I'm about to have a little breakfast of my own, and when I'm done, we're leavin', whether you're finished or not."

As Dane ate his breakfast and drank his coffee, he studied Sheriff Woodridge's rogues' gallery, aware that the sheriff was still glaring at him from behind. After a moment or two Dane turned toward the sheriff.

"I don't reckon it matters none to you that half a dozen or more of these fellas are dead already," he said.

"You kill 'em?"

"Some of them," Dane said.

"How does it feel, Calder, makin' a livin' by killin' folk?"

"I don't kill for a living, Sheriff," Dane replied evenly. "When I can, I take them in. If I'm forced to kill someone, it's his choice. And I can live with that a lot better than I could live with being a sheriff who has sworn to protect the public but who has sold out to the outlaws."

"I haven't sold out to anybody," Woodridge said resolutely. He pointed to his rogues' gallery. "You think any of those men have given me money not to arrest them?"

"It doesn't matter whether you've taken any money from them or not. You've sold out to them just to buy a little peace in your town." Dane turned up his cup and swallowed the last of his coffee. "But that's your problem, not mine," he said. He set his empty cup on the sheriff's desk. "I'll get these two out of your hair."

Dane walked over to the wall hook and took down the key ring.

"Calder?" Woodridge called. Dane stopped and looked toward the sheriff. Woodridge ran his hand through his hair, then adjusted the bandage around his head. "Watch out on the trail," he said. "I heard some talk."

"What sort of talk?"

"A few of the boys got together last night," he said. "They figure if they can kill you and free your two prisoners, it'll be a sign to all the other bounty hunters and lawmen that Loma Alta should be left alone."

"Thanks for the warning," Dane said.

"Yeah. Well, I'll be honest with you. If they get the job done, I ain't goin' to lose no sleep over it," Woodridge said. "But bushwhackin' a man on the trail...that's goin' too far, even for me."

"Do you have any idea where this is supposed to happen?"

"No," Woodridge said. "I told you all I know. The rest is up to you."

DANE RODE behind Charley and Babbit, using his proven method of securing them to each other and to him by hangman's nooses. To be honest, he wasn't one-hundred-percent certain that the nooses would really break their necks if they attempted to run. This was because the fear the nooses instilled in his prisoners was great enough that no one had ever tried it.

They crossed a little stream and Dane watched the hooves kick up silver sprays of water as they went across.

"Hey," Babbit called. "Let's stop here for water."

"We've got enough water in our canteens," Dane said.

"The water in our canteens tastes sour," Babbit said. "This will be good cold water."

Babbit was right. The stream was swiftly running and cool and it would be good. And the water in their canteens was tepid and sour. But if they stopped here, it might well be Dane's last stop. That was because for some time now Dane had been aware that three men were dogging them, riding parallel with them and for the most part staying out of sight. This would be a perfect spot for them to try their ambush if they were going to. Dane didn't plan to give them that opportunity.

"I think my horse is gong lame," Charley said a short while later.

"Do you?"

"Yeah, can't you see him? He's favorin' his left foreleg somethin' awful."

"Not that I can see," Dane said.

"Well, then, you're blind," Charley said. "We've got to stop. We've got to stop, I tell you, and give him a rest. Maybe he's just picked up a stone or something."

Since both men had tried to make him stop, Dane knew then that they were aware that an ambush was being planned. They were doing all in their power to give the bushwhackers every opportunity to be successful.

Dane looked over to his left without being obvious about it and saw three riders slipping through a notch in the hills, moving so quietly and expertly that only someone who was specifically looking for them would have noticed.

Ahead of them was a narrow draw. While they were in the draw they would be protected, but when they emerged from the other end, they would for a while be totally exposed, while any would-be ambushers would have the cover of an outcropping of rocks. Dane knew that the ambush would take place at this spot, but he had no idea what he was going to do to thwart it.

Then, as soon as they entered the draw, Dane ordered them to stop.

"Stop? What for?" Charley asked.

"You said you were afraid your horse was going lame. Here's your chance to take a look at him," Dane suggested.

"Yeah, well, now I don't think it was anything," Charley replied. "I think he just picked up a small stone, then threw it, that's all. He's doin' fine now."

"Stop anyway," Dane said, giving a small jerk on the rope.

"All right, all right!" Charley complained. "Be careful with that rope. You're goin' to break our necks if you don't watch out."

"No," Dane said. "I'm goin' to break your neck if *you* don't watch out."

The two prisoners climbed down. Charley started to go through the motions of looking at his horse's hoof.

"Don't bother with that," Dane said.

"What?"

"There's nothing wrong with your horse. You know it and I know it."

"Then why did we stop?"

"Because I want to change shirts and hats with you."

"What? Why would you want to do that?"

"Because I like your shirt better."

"You're crazy," Charley said. He started to get back onto his horse, but he was stopped when he heard the metallic click of Dane's pistol being cocked.

"Maybe you didn't hear me. I said take off your shirt and hat," Dane repeated.

"Now that just don't make no sense at all. And anyhow I can't. My hands are cuffed."

Dane held up the key and motioned Charley toward him. Puzzled by Dane's strange request, Charley moved toward him, holding out his hands. Dane released the handcuffs, then Dane, and then Charley began taking off their shirts.

"What about me?" Babbit said. "Don't I get to get naked, too?"

"Your turn will come," Dane said.

"My turn will come? My turn will come for what? What the hell has got into you?" Babbit asked.

"Don't worry about it," Dane said. "I'll tell you what you need to know when you need to know it."

A moment later Charley had put on Dane's shirt and started to get back on his horse.

"No," Dane said. "Ride this horse for a while."

"Would you mind tellin' me just what the hell you're a doin'?" Charley asked.

"Mount up," Dane said. "You ride back there. I'll ride up here with Babbit."

"This don't make no sense," Charley mumbled as he mounted Dane's horse.

Remounted, the men rode through the long narrow draw toward the bright wedge of light at the far end. The horses' hooves clattered loudly against the stone and the echoes tumbling back to them make it sound as if an entire troop of men were riding through instead of only three.

"No!" he shouted out loud. "No, don't shoot! Don't shoot!"

"Charley, what the hell's got into you?" Babbit asked.

"Don't you see what this son of a bitch has done?" Charley shouted. "He's got me wearin' his duds an' ridin' his horse! Darnell! Garcia! Townsend! Don't shoot! It's me, Charley!" •

One of the three bushwhackers stood up about one hundred yards up the trail. He could be seen from the waist up, but only in silhouette against the bright sky.

"All right, Calder," the bushwhacker called. "You pulled a pretty good one on us this time. But you got a long way to go, and I don't think you're goin' to get there."

The silhouette disappeared, and a moment later, Dane heard the clatter of horses being ridden at a gallop.

"You think you're so damned smart," Charley said. "They'll just find someplace else. And this time they won't be fooled by changing shirts and horses."

"Charley," Dane said, giving the rope one more good tug. Charley let out a choking sound. "You talk too damned much."

16

Townsend lay on the top of the flat rock, looking back along the trail over which they had just come. He saw the three riders moving slowly but steadily to the north. From this distance he had no idea which one of the three might be Calder, but it didn't matter. Even if he did know, he was much too far out of range to do anything about it.

Behind him, Darnell and Garcia sat resting. Darnell was chewing on the root of a grass stem. Garcia had his boot off, examining a blister.

"You see 'em?" Darnell asked.

"Yeah. They're 'bout a mile behind us."

"You figured out who is who yet?"

"No," Townsend admitted. "Even if I did, there ain't no place we could set up an ambush between there and here. And I sure as hell don't plan to go out into the open to take him on."

"Why not? There's five of us and only one of him."

"Where do you get five?" Garcia asked. It was the

first time he had spoken, as he had been too interested in the blister on his toe.

"Well, you gotta count Babbit and Charley Redford as bein' on our side," Darnell said.

"Why? What the hell can they do? They ain't even armed."

"Well, I don't know. They can do somethin'," Darnell said. "Get in the way so he can't get off a shot, or somethin'."

"They'll get in the way, all right. They'll get themselves killed and us, too," Garcia said. "If we get another chance at an ambush like before, I say we ought to do it."

"I know the country from here to Coyote Springs," Townsend said. "We won't get another chance like the one we just had."

"Yeah? Well, maybe there is another place," Darnell suggested.

"Where?" Garcia asked as, wincing in pain, he put his boots back on. "'Cause what I'd like to do is kill this son of a bitch and get it over with."

"There ain't no way he's goin' to get back to Coyote Springs without goin' through Three Wells, and there ain't no way he's goin' through there without stoppin' for the night. We'll be waitin' for him there."

"Yeah," Garcia said, smiling broadly. "Yeah, that's a good idea. And maybe we can have a few drinks while we wait."

To PREVENT any ambush on the trail Dane had Charley and Babbit change shirts and hats a couple more times so that anyone watching from a distance would be thoroughly confused as to who was who. By the time they approached Three Wells, however, they were back in their proper attire.

As they rode by boot hill they saw four fresh graves. One of them was the grave of Hawk Doyle.

"I see you killed poor Hawk," Charley said.

Dane shook his head. "No," he said. "Rafe Cassidy shot him, but you're the one killed him, Charley. All I'm doing is collecting the reward."

"You're a coldhearted man, you know that?" Charley said. "I mean, to take advantage of another man's misery like that."

"The reward was there, the body was there," Dane said. "If I don't collect on it, someone else will."

As the three men rode toward the jail, the fact that two of them were connected by noosed rope caught the attention of many of the townspeople.

"Hey! It's Dane Calder!" someone called.

"Calder's back, and he has Redford and Babbit with him!"

"I knew them boys wouldn't get away from that bounty hunter."

As the shouted news traveled from one to another, a crowd began to build and the crowd followed the horsemen down the street, running along on the boardwalk, or hurrying through the dirt. Several young boys, using bent twigs as toy guns, shot at each other as they hurried along.

"Bang, bang! I'm Dane Calder and you're Charley Redford and you're dead! Bang, bang!"

"No! I'm Dane Calder and you're Charley Redford!"

"I don't want to be Charley Redford. Charley Redford is going to hang."

"So's Nathan Babbit."

"Wish they'd do it here so we could watch, don't you?"

Charley, who couldn't help but overhear the shouted argument, stared straight ahead and licked his lips nervously.

Calder chuckled. "What's the matter, Charley? You're looking a little peaked."

"Them kids," Charley growled. "Somebody ought to teach 'em some manners."

By the time they reached the jail, Sheriff Grimes was standing on the front porch, smiling.

"Well, Calder, you come back to pay us another visit, I see."

"Can you keep these two for me overnight?" Dane asked, swinging down from his horse.

"Be glad to," Grimes said. "Come on, you two, we got a nice quiet cell just waitin' for you."

"Have 'em ready to go by sunup, would you, Sheriff?"

"They'll be ready. Why don't you head on down to the saloon? Doc, Louis, Ken, Matt, and the others are plannin' on givin' you all you can eat and drink, I think."

"Thanks," Dane said. "Maybe I'll just do that."

When Dane stepped into the saloon a few minutes later, Belle was actually the first one to greet him. She slid her arm through his and escorted him over to the same table where he had played cards with Doc and the others a few days earlier. A pitcher of beer and a clean glass was already there, and no sooner had he sat down than someone brought him a plate of beans.

"We got you a steak cookin' too, if you want it," Louis said.

"Steak sounds good," Dane admitted. He picked up the fork. "And the beans smell good," he added, taking a bite.

In the far corner of the same saloon, Darnell, Garcia, and Townsend sat nursing a whiskey.

"Look at the way they gather around him," Townsend said. "You'd think the son of a bitch was just like Abraham Lincoln or somebody."

"Maybe he is," Darnell said.

"What are you talkin' about, maybe he is?"

Darnell looked at the other two and smiled. "Well, as I recollect, Lincoln got shot, didn't he?"

Townsend and Garcia laughed out loud.

"Yeah," Garcia said. "Yeah, he did at that."

"Let's drink a toast to old Abe," Darnell offered, and laughing, the other two held their glasses out and joined in the toast.

Dane ate and drank his fill that evening, though he begged out of a repeat of the card game with the excuse that he was tired and had a lot of distance to cover the next day. "I'm going to get the biggest bed in the quietest room in the hotel," he told the others. "And I'm going to sleep the sleep of the dead."

"D'ya hear that?" Darnell asked. "Calder wants to sleep the sleep of the dead."

"Well, we'll just have to see if we can help him out," Garcia replied.

Dane waved goodbye to his well-wishers in the saloon, then walked over to the hotel. He asked for, and got, the room overlooking the street.

"Will you require a knock on your door to awaken you, Mr. Calder?" the desk clerk asked.

"I'll probably wake myself," Calder said as he signed the guest registration book. "But if you haven't seen me by sunup, give me a yell."

"Yes, sir, Mr. Calder. It'll be my pleasure."

Dane climbed the stairs then started down the long corridor toward his room. The corridor was well lighted with wall-mounted gas lanterns, which heated and filled the hallway with their quiet hissing sound. Once Dane was in his room and with the door closed behind him, it was dark, cool, and inviting. The window was open and a gentle night breeze lifted the gauze curtains.

Dane lit the lantern alongside his bed, took his gun belt off, then stepped up to the open window and looked out onto the dark street below. From here he could see the side of the jail and the small, barred window of the cell where Sheriff Grimes had put his prisoners. He saw no one, but it was dark inside the cell, so even if someone was standing at the window, he wouldn't have been able to see them. He yawned and stretched, then went over to extinguish the lamp and plunge his room into darkness.

"THERE!" Darnell said. "Did you see the son of a bitch standing there in his window, just as cool as you please?

"Yeah, I saw him," Garcia said. "You'd think he'd have better sense than to stand there like that. Why, if we'da had a rifle, we coulda picked him off like shootin' a fish in a barrel."

"And if a frog had wings, he wouldn't bump his ass ever' time he jumps," Darnell growled. "Come on, let's go down to the jail and have a talk with Charley and Babbit."

The three men walked back to the rear of the saloon, then moved along behind the row of buildings toward the jail. They were assailed by unpleasant odors, from stale beer, to privies, to garbage dumps of rotted food, though they were odors of such familiarity that the men scarcely noticed.

"There it is," Darnell said when they reached the rear of the barbershop.

The three men moved quickly across the narrow space between the barbershop and the jail, then stood up against the wall of the jail. Here the shadows and darkness shielded them from view, even if someone had been walking down the street right in front of the jail.

"Hey!" Townsend called. "Hey, Babbit! Redford! You in there?"

Babbit's face appeared in the window of the cell. "Yeah, we're here," Babbit said. "Where you guys been? We ain't seen you since early this mornin'."

"I know. After Calder pulled that trick on us, we didn't get another chance," Townsend said. "Until now."

"Now? What are you goin' to do now?" Charley asked, his face joining Babbit's in the cell window.

"Calder's took him a room over to the hotel," Townsend explained. "Soon's we're sure he's asleep good, we're goin' to go over and take care of him, once and for all."

"Forget about him," Charley said. "Get us out of here."

"Not yet."

"What do you mean not yet?" Charley hissed. "Dammit, Calder's plannin' on takin' us back to hang! Get us out of here!"

"If we get you out before we get Calder, he'll just come after us all," Townsend said. "And I don't want that buzzard on my tail."

"He's right, Charley," Babbit said. "Calder's like a bulldog. Once he gets hold of you, he don't let go. I know that better'n anybody."

"Well, get us out of here and we'll help you get him," Charley said.

"Huh-uh," Townsend said, shaking his head. "Me an' Darnell an' Garcia done talked it over. If we get you out now, Calder's liable to hear the commotion and we'll lose our chance at him. I'm tellin' you, right now is the best chance there's ever been to kill him."

"Yeah," Darnell added. "And think what all we can do once Calder is dead. Hell, we can prob'ly get a reward from just about ever'one that's on the dodge."

"All right, all right," Charley agreed reluctantly. "I want him dead just as much as anyone...prob'ly more'n most people. But don't leave us to rot here once you get the job done."

"Don't worry, you won't be rottin' here. Once we get the job done, this town will be ours," Townsend promised.

"When you goin' to do it?"

"'Bout midnight. Right now we're goin' to go back and have a few drinks to while away the time. Then, 'bout midnight, we'll mosey on over to the hotel and do the job."

"Listen for the shots," Garcia added. "When you hear the shots, you'll know it's us, takin' care of business."

17

The girl got up from the bed and walked over to the washstand, where she poured water into a large porcelain basin. When she saw Garcia staring at her, she picked up the basin and went behind the dressing screen.

"What the hell did you do that for?" Garcia asked.

"There are some things a girl needs to do in private," she answered. There was a ripple of water as she dipped the washcloth into the basin.

"You ain't a girl, you're a whore," Garcia said gruffly. "And since I paid for your time, there ain't none of it private. Now take down that screen."

There was another rippling sound of water, but the screen stayed up.

"I said, take down that there screen!" Garcia shouted, and he got out of bed and knocked the dressing screen across the room. It hit the wall, then splintered.

The girl let out a quick shout of fear, then cringed, frightened that he was about to hit her.

"I ain't goin' to hit you," he said. "I'm just goin' to watch. Now go on about your business."

The girl, sobbing silently in fear and embarrassment, dipped the cloth in the water and continued her ablutions. There was a loud knock on the door.

"Belle? Belle, you all right?" a man's voice called.

"Don't you worry none about the little girlie," Garcia called back. "She's just fine."

"Belle?" the voice called again.

"Go on about your business," Garcia said. "I told you the girl is just fine."

"I want to hear her voice," the man outside the door insisted.

Garcia walked over to his pants and pulled his pistol from his holster. He pointed it at the door and cocked it.

"I ain't a-goin' to tell you no more," he said.

"No, Don't!" Belle shouted. "Smokey, it's all right! I'm fine."

"You sure? I thought I heard you yell," Smokey's voice called from the other side of the door.

"It's all right, really," Belle said. "I...I knocked over the dressing screen by accident, that's all."

"All right," Smokey said reluctantly. "But you call me if you need me."

"Go on back to your drinkin' cowboy," Garcia said. "And let us get back to our business." He laughed mockingly.

"I'll...I'll be downstairs," Smokey said.

Belle stood up.

"What are you doin'?" Garcia asked.

"I'm finished," she said.

"You're finished? That's all there is to it?"

Belle nodded.

"Hell, what was you so private about? You didn't do nothin' but splash a little water onto yourself."

"Do you want me to bathe you?" she asked.

"What?" Garcia asked, covering himself indignantly. "No! I took me a bath not no more'n a few days ago. I done it all by myself. And if and when I need another'n, why, I'll take that one by myself, too. Fact is, why'n't you just turn your back now an' let me get dressed?"

"Whatever you say," Belle said, waiting until she turned before she smiled at his sudden case of modesty.

───────

GARCIA WAS STILL PACKING his shirttail down in his pants as he came down the stairs to join Darnell and Townsend.

"How was she?" Townsend asked.

"You want to know how she was, you spend your own money," Garcia said.

"Don't need to," Townsend said. "I figure you'll pay for it, then you won't be able to keep quiet about it. Pretty soon you'll be talkin' about it so much we won't be able to get you to shut up."

"You don't say," Garcia replied. "Well, I ain't talkin' yet. What time is it?" he asked.

Darnell pointed to the clock on the wall behind the bar. "Accordin' to that, it's near on to midnight," he said.

"You think he's asleep yet?"

"I reckon he is. He had a hard day and he figures to get up early for another hard day tomorrow. I reckon he's asleep by now."

Garcia smiled, then loosed the pistol in his holster. "Then what do you say we pay the great bounty hunter a visit?"

Garcia, Darnell, and Townsend left the saloon, then slipped quickly and quietly through the dark of night to the front of the hotel. There, they stopped.

"Look around," Darnell whispered. "You see if the sheriff or one of his deputies is makin' rounds?"

"I don't see nobody," Townsend replied.

"All right, let's go in."

The lobby was lighted by only one small lamp, so it was fairly dark. It was deserted as well, for the scattering of chairs and sofas that were sometimes occupied by guests were all empty. Only the night clerk was in the lobby and he was sitting in a chair behind the desk. His chair was tipped back and his head was slumped forward. His chest was rising and falling in rhythm with his snores.

"Get your guns out, gents, and be quiet," Darnell said, pulling his own pistol.

With guns drawn, they slipped through the shadows of the lobby, then started up the stairs. When they reached the landing, Darnell held his finger to his lips. Here, the light was so bright they had to squint.

"Get those damned lights out!" Darnell ordered, and Townsend moved quickly down the corridor, extinguishing each lamp until the hallway was a long tunnel of darkness.

"Come on," Townsend said. "That's his door down there."

The three men moved silently through the dark hall until they were just outside the door.

"Shall we break it in?" Garcia asked.

"I don't know," Darnell replied. "If we don't get it the first time, he'll hear the commotion and we'll be sittin' ducks out here."

"How else we goin' to get in?" Garcia wanted to know.

"Why don't we just try the doorknob?" Townsend suggested, turning it slowly.

"You stupid or somethin'? You think he'd be crazy enough to leave it unlocked?" Garcia asked.

The door swung open.

"Would you look at that? He didn't even lock it," Darnell said, voicing the surprise of all of them.

"Go on in."

The room was slightly brighter than the hallway, because of the pale moonlight that fell in through the open window. They could see the bed and Calder's hat and pistol belt, hanging from the brass bedpost.

"This is goin' to be like takin' candy from a baby," Darnell said, aiming at the bed.

Darnell fired and his shot was followed almost immediately by the other two, so that, for a moment, all three guns were firing, lighting up the darkness with white flashes and filling the room with thunder.

After they had fired three shots apiece, Darnell shouted to stop firing. "The whole town will be in here in a minute. We got to get out of here," he said. "Check and make sure he's dead!"

Townsend walked over to the bed and felt around, then gasped in surprise. "Darnell! He ain't here!" he shouted.

"What? Where is he?"

"I'm right here," Dane said. He was standing on the porch roof, just outside his window.

With shouts of frustrated rage and fear, all three would-be assassins turned their guns toward the window and began firing. Bullets crashed through the window, sending large shards of glass out onto the porch roof. Dane had jumped to one side of the window as soon as he spoke, so he avoided the initial fusillade. After the first volley he leaned around and fired into the room. He hit one of the men and saw him go down. The other two bolted through the door.

At first Dane planned to go after them by climbing back into the room, but he decided to just wait until they were on the street. There, they would have fewer places to hide...and there would be less likelihood of an innocent bystander being hurt.

Dane, who had been sleeping on the porch roof, fully clothed, ran to the edge of the roof, then jumped down into the space between the hotel and the building next door. He waited there in the shadows and kept his eyes on the front door of the hotel. As he expected, the door burst open a moment later and two men ran out. Dane stepped out into the street to brace them.

"Hold it right there!" he called to them.

"It's Calder!" one of the two men shouted, and he fired.

The bullet whizzed by Dane's ear, much closer than was comfortable, and Dane returned fire, shooting above and just to the right of the shooter's flame pattern. He heard a grunt of pain.

The lone survivor darted across the street and disappeared into the darkness on the other side.

Crouching low, Dane moved back into the darkness on his side of the street, then began searching, trying to find his quarry. A door opened from somewhere behind him and one of the townspeople came out, carrying a rifle. It was Dr. Andrews.

"What's goin' on? Did Babbit and Redford escape?"

"No," Dane said. "But a few of their friends are tryin' to get 'em out."

The assailant fired from the shadows on the other side of the street and his bullet hit the post between Dane and Doc, sending pieces of wooden splinters into their faces.

"Damn, that hurt!" Doc said.

"Get back in the shadows, Doc," Dane said. "No sense in you gettin' hurt."

"I just want to help."

"You won't be helpin' anyone by gettin' yourself killed."

Suddenly a horse burst out of the shadows from across the street, and its rider, bending low, began firing toward Dane.

Dane shot back, missing the rider, but hitting a lit kerosene lantern that hung on a piece of wood sticking out over the street from the corner of the leather-goods store. Dane's bullet burst the kerosene tank and sent the fuel up into the lighted chimney, causing the lantern to explode. When it did so, it sent a shower of flaming kerosene onto the rider's back.

"Ahhhhhieee!" the rider screamed in terror and pain as he galloped down the street, flaming now like a human torch.

Dane reached for Doc's rifle, jacked a round into the chamber, then raised it to his shoulder. He took a long, careful aim at the ball of fire that had now panicked his horse into galloping faster than ever. By now the outlaw was at the far end of the street, better than two hundred yards away.

Dane squeezed the trigger, and the rifle fired, then kicked back against his shoulder. At the far end of the street the fleeing, flaming, rider pitched out of his saddle with a bullet in the back of his head, dead before he ever hit the dirt. He lay there on the ground, burning for several seconds, until a couple of the citizens from that end of town, having been awakened by the commotion, hurried out into the street to douse the flames.

By now Sheriff Grimes was on the scene, wearing

pants, boots, and his undershirt. He hadn't even bothered to strap on his pistol, though he was carrying a rifle.

"What happened?" he asked.

"Some men tried to bushwhack Calder, here," Doc explained.

"Locals?" the sheriff asked in surprise.

Dane shook his head. "They were from Loma Alta," he explained. "They tried earlier today. I thought they might try again tonight, so I was ready for them." He pointed to the body lying nearby in the street, already drawing a crowd of curious onlookers. "There's one there," he said. "There's another up in my room, and that one down there."

Sheriff Grimes shook his head and chuckled. "Ready for them, huh? I guess you were."

18

Three Wells had telegraphed ahead the news that Dane Calder would be arriving with Charley Redford and Nathan Babbit, so when the three men rode into Coyote Springs, the entire town had turned out to meet them.

"Did they give you much of a fight, Calder?" someone called.

"Hey, Cactus Charley, you think you'll get away this time?"

"I'll be comin' to your dance, Charley!"

Charley stared ahead glumly, and when they reached the jail, Sheriff McQuade and Judge Sweeny were standing there on the porch to meet them.

"Well, Charley, welcome home," Sheriff McQuade said.

"You go to hell," Charley snarled.

"Now, that's no way to be," McQuade said.

"I hope you got somethin' to eat in there," Charley said. "That son of a bitch ain't fed us nothin' but jerky for three days." Charley started toward the front door of the jailhouse, but Sheriff McQuade reached out his hand to stop him.

"Huh-uh, Charley, you won't be goin' in there," he said.

"What do you mean?"

"Boys, take him over to the courtyard and put him in the holding cell."

"The holding cell?" Charley said in dread. "No! What are you goin' to put me in there for?"

"Why, Charley, don't you remember?" McQuade said. "That's where you were headed when you escaped."

"Yeah, but you don't go there until just before you hang. What is this, a lynchin'? Don't I even get a trial first?"

"You've had your trial," Judge Sweeny replied. "There's no need to try you again. You were found guilty, you were sentenced to hang, and hang you shall, this very afternoon."

"Babbit, do somethin'," Charley said as a couple of deputies led him toward the courthouse. "They're fixin' to hang me!"

"Charley, boy, if I was you, I wouldn't be worryin' none 'bout the hangin'," Babbit said. "I'd be worryin' 'bout what you're goin' to say to Wes Boone, and Clay Morrow, and Hawk Doyle when you run into 'em down in hell. You know, you just left them boys to die, and I don't reckon they're goin' to treat you too kindly when they see you again."

"You...you left 'em, too," Charley said.

"Maybe so, but they wasn't my gang—they was yours," Babbit replied. "Besides which, I ain't goin' to hang this afternoon. You are."

"You bastard! I'll see you in hell!" Charley shouted as they took him away.

Babbit began to laugh.

"I don't know what you have to laugh about, mister," Sheriff McQuade said. "I figure we'll have you tried tomorrow mornin' and hung by tomorrow afternoon."

"Yeah? Well, I ain't got no rope around my neck yet. And you can ask the bounty hunter here, I ain't that easy to hold on to. Tell him, Calder. Tell him!" Babbit said, with a mocking laugh.

"Babbit, most of the time I turn you people in, collect the money, then leave. But this time I'm going to stay around to watch you hang. And if the sheriff's arm is sore, I might even pull the handle myself."

"I'll have the money ready for you this afternoon," Judge Sweeny said.

"Soon enough," Dane replied. "I'd like to take a bath, get a good, hot meal, then a hotel room. If I'm goin' to wait around to see Babbit hang, I'm going to wait in comfort."

"You'll never see me hang," Babbit taunted.

"Get him inside," Judge Sweeny ordered and Sheriff McQuade and the remaining deputy escorted Babbit into the jail.

By two o'clock in the afternoon, Dane had bathed, put on a clean shirt and pants, and was in Judge Sweeny's office for his money.

"I've got it right here for you," Judge Sweeny said, taking it out of his desk drawer. "The reward I promised you for Redford, plus the reward that was already posted for Morrow and Doyle. And I must tell you, I have never paid out a reward with more pleasure. That is one bunch of men I am glad to see gone." He counted out the money, then handed it to Dane.

"Thanks," Dane said. "What time will Babbit's trial be tomorrow?"

"Nine in the morning," Judge Sweeny said. "We'll hang him at two."

"I'll be here."

Judge Sweeny stroked his chin. "You know, you got paid quite a bit more for Charley Redford and his bunch than you did for Babbit. Yet I get the distinct feeling you got more satisfaction from bringing him in than all the others put together."

"I did."

"Why?"

"I saw the girl," Dane said.

"The girl? Oh, yes, you mean the Indian girl he mutilated. Yes, I suppose that was a grisly scene."

"I knew her," Dane added.

"I see. Then that would make it worse. Well, Mr. Calder, I not only congratulate you, I commend you for not letting your personal feelings get in the way of doing your job. I know you were tempted to kill Babbit yourself, and under the circumstances, if you had done it, you would probably have gotten away with it. I admire your respect for the law."

Dane smiled dryly. "Respect for the law has nothing to do with it," he said. "I never met anyone yet who wouldn't rather be shot than hanged."

There was a knock on the door and Judge Sweeny yelled for whoever it was to come in. It was his law clerk.

"Judge," the clerk said. "They got Charley Redford standin' on the gallows. The sheriff is waitin' for your signal."

"Yes," Judge Sweeny said. He sighed and looked up at Dane. "You know, Mr. Calder, I can sentence someone to die...and in the case of a person like Charley Redford...a cold-blooded murderer, I can do it with a clear conscience. But when it comes to the part where I actually have to give the signal to dispatch the soul of another human being into eternity...I must confess to having qualms." He walked over to the window. "Come, watch with me," he said. "After all, you have a hand in this too."

Dane walked over to the window and looked down into the courtyard. Three or four hundred people had gathered around the gallows. There were reporters and a photographer in the front row, though since Charley had just been brought in that same morning, the reporters were local only, there being insufficient time to gather any from the national newspapers.

Charley was standing just under the cross beam with the noose around his neck and a hood over his face. His hands were manacled to his belt, so that his arms were stiffly by his sides. His legs were tied together. Any last words he may have had were already spoken at this point, and he was quietly counting off the last seconds of his life.

Judge Sweeny nodded, and down on the gallows, Sheriff McQuade, who had been awaiting the signal, pulled the handle. From his position at the open window in Judge Sweeny's office, Dane could hear the thump of the dropping trapdoor, then the oohs and aahs of the assembled crowd. Charley Redford dropped straight and true, turned one-half turn to the left, then was very still.

———

THOUGH THE SUN was a full disk up in the east, Dane was still sound asleep when he was awakened by a loud banging on his hotel room door. He sat up quickly, drawing his gun from the holster that hung on the bedstead.

"What is it?" he shouted gruffly.

"Calder, it's me, Sheriff McQuade. Open up."

Still holding his gun, Dane walked over to the door and opened it slightly, just to make certain the sheriff was alone. When he saw that he was alone, he opened it all the way.

"Yeah, come on in," he invited. He took his pants off the back of the chair and started putting them on. As he did so he saw the look of agitation on the sheriff's face. "Babbit?" he asked.

"Yes. How did you know?"

"Just a hunch."

"When I came to the office this morning, I found my night deputy lying dead, just outside the cell. His throat had been cut. Evidently Babbit lured him over to the cell for some notion, then managed to cut his throat and get the keys."

"You seem to have a hell of a time holding on to your prisoners, Sheriff," Dane said.

"I...I can't deny that," McQuade said. "I don't know where he got the knife. We searched him thoroughly before we put him in the cell."

"Babbit is a pretty resourceful man," Dane said. "He probably made the knife out of something he found in the cell."

"Maybe so. Well, he's well-armed and well mounted. He took a pistol and holster from the office."

Dane pulled on his boots, then strapped on his gun. "So am I," he said.

"Then you're going after him? You'll bring him back?"

"You asked two questions, Sheriff," Dane replied. "And I'm only going to answer the first one. Yes."

19

THREE DAYS LATER

A t first Dane thought that Babbit would head for Loma Alta, but it was soon obvious he had another destination in mind. It was still south—Babbit hadn't changed his mind about going into Mexico, though there was always the possibility that he wouldn't even make it to the border. All the indications were that he was pushing his horse at a killing pace.

Dane, on the other hand, rode easily, sparingly, knowing that in the long run he would make just as good time because his horse would still be fresh while Babbit's horse was wearing out. On the third day Dane got close enough to get a glimpse of Babbit in the distance. That was when he knew the killer was heading for Rio Lobo, another one of the little towns on the American side of the border.

Dane arrived in Rio Lobo just about suppertime,

and along with the spicy aromas of Mexican cooking, he could smell coffee, pork chops, fried potatoes, and baking bread.

"Yara? Yara?" a woman called, and Dane, startled because that had been the name of the Indian girl Babbit had mutilated, jerked his horse to a halt to look in the direction of the call.

"Si, signora?" a young Mexican girl answered.

"Take the clothes down from the line," the woman ordered.

"Si, signora," the servant girl replied.

The woman, startled by the fact that Dane had stopped his horse, looked at him nervously, and, instinctively, took a step backward. Dane touched the brim of his hat in greeting, then urged his horse on.

A game of checkers was being played by two gray-bearded men in front of the feed store, watched over by half a dozen kibitzers. A couple of them looked up at Dane as he rode by, his horse's hooves clumping hollowly on the hard-packed earth of the street. None of them seemed to recognize him, which was good, because Dane didn't exactly want his presence announced.

The shopkeeper who was running the dry goods store came through his front door and began vigorously sweeping the wooden porch. His broom did little but raise the dust to swirl about, then fall back down again. He brushed a sleeping dog off the porch, but even before he went back inside, the dog reclaimed his position, curled around comfortably, and within a moment was asleep again.

Dane saw the horse from the far end of the street. As he had known from the trail, the animal had been ridden nearly to death, and even at a distance Dane could see that he was totally defeated.

Dane rode slowly down to the far end of the street, then tied his horse to a hitch rail next to the poor animal. He walked over to the horse and patted it on the neck. The horse's coat was smeared with foam and it was breathing in labored gasps. Its muzzle and the hitch rail were flecked with blood that had spewed from its mouth and nostrils by the painful breaths. It had been ridden until its lungs burst.

For a moment Dane felt a savage rage at a person who could do that to a horse.

Dane sighed, then pulled his pistol and aimed it at the horse's head. The horse looked toward him, his big brown eyes sad and knowing. He nodded once, almost as if telling Dane that he understood what had to be done. Then the horse looked away and waited stoically for the release from its suffering. Dane pulled the trigger and the horse fell to the ground. The gunshot echoed through the quiet streets for a long time. Then it was silent.

The gunshot attracted several of the townspeople. They looked toward the saloon, at the man with the smoking gun, and at the horse that lay motionless on the street.

A curtain fluttered in one of the false fronts.

A cat yowled somewhere down the street.

A fly buzzed past Dane's ear, did a few circles, then descended quickly to the horse, joined almost immediately by a dozen others, drawn to the unexpected feast.

Dane pushed through the bat-wing doors, then stepped to one side so that a wall was at this back. At the bar, a glass of beer in front of him, his lips dripping with moisture, stood Nathan Babbit.

Dane's lips twisted into an evil smile. Part of him wanted to kill the man this instant, while part of him wanted to delay the pleasure. He remembered the fear Charley Redford had shown toward hanging, and he wanted Babbit to know that same terror. Maybe he would take him back.

"Babbit," Dane said. His words were cold, flat, menacing.

Babbit didn't turn around, didn't even look at him in the mirror. Instead he stared into his glass of beer with those cold, droopy eyes.

"Well, look who's here. I would've thought you'd give up on me by now."

"I've come for you, Babbit."

There were half a dozen drinkers at the bar, and at Dane's words, they hurried to move away. Tables and chairs scooted across the floor as everyone in the saloon got up and moved back against the wall, out of the line of fire.

Dane caught the movement of the others out of the corner of his eye. He was pretty sure Babbit had not picked up any partners in his short flight of freedom, but he wanted to be certain. A quick glance was all it took to convince him that there was no one else who represented any danger to him.

Babbit still did not turn around. "What was that shooting out front?" he asked.

"I had to shoot your horse."

"You shouldn't have done that. That was a good horse."

"Not after you got through with him, you horse-killing bastard."

"Well, he wasn't my horse anyway. I just borrowed him when I left," Babbit said with a low, evil laugh.

"You disappointed a few folks back there, Babbit. They were wanting to see you dance."

"I thought I'd just let old Charley do all the dancin' for me."

"Charley did his show. Now it's your turn."

"No, thank you. I got no plans to go hang."

"I don't give a damn what your plans are, Babbit. You're going back and you're going to hang."

"If you're so all-fired set on seein' me dead, Calder, why don't you just shoot me here and be done with it?"

"Huh-uh," Dane said. "Shooting you is too good for you. I saw the way Charley sweated before he was hanged. I don't intend to deny myself the pleasure of seeing you go through the same thing."

Babbit turned away from the bar to look at Dane. He was smiling evilly.

"You know, Calder, I used to wonder why you kept on doggin' me when there was others with higher prices on their heads. Then someone told me that you took it real personal what me and Turner did to that Indian girl. They said you know'd her. Is that right?"

"I knew her," Dane said.

"That's why you kept comin', huh?"

"That's why."

"Then you seen what I did to her," Babbit said.

Dane's first reaction was of revulsion, then he saw that Babbit was using bringing up Yara as a diversionary tactic. He saw Babbit's hand snake down to his side to draw his pistol.

Dane reacted to the sudden move quickly, drawing his own pistol faster than he had ever drawn it before, spurred on in the effort by a year of controlled rage toward this man. He had his own gun out in time to take quick but deliberate aim and shoot Babbit in the gut. Babbit, the barrel of his own pistol just topping the holster, pulled the trigger, shooting lead into the floor. A red stain began to spread just over his belt buckle.

Babbit's gun clattered to the floor and he put his hands over his belly wound and watched the blood spill through his fingers. Inexplicably, he smiled.

"You're fast, Calder," he said. "Faster'n I thought." He weaved back and forth for a moment, then pitched forward, crashing through a table before landing on the floor.

Smoke from the discharge of the weapons formed a big cloud, then began to drift toward the ceiling.

Dane kneeled beside Babbit. The outlaw was still alive.

"This isn't how I wanted you to die, Babbit," he said. "I wanted to take you back. I wanted to see you hang."

Babbit tried to laugh, but it came out a barking cough. Little flecks of blood sprayed out onto his lips and his shirt.

"I reckon I beat you after all," he rasped. "I told you I wasn't goin' to hang."

"Not quite," Dane said. He stood up and rammed his pistol back in his holster. "Dead's dead, I reckon."

The bat-wings swung open and a man with a badge came inside. His hair and mustache were gray, his face lined around his blue eyes. There was a sharpness to his eyes that told Dane the peace officer had probably been pretty good when he was younger. Only age had driven him to a backwater place like Rio Lobo, where little happened. Age had undoubtedly slowed him down, but Dane imagined there were still a few who could make the mistake of misjudging him. Dane didn't intend to make that mistake.

"You shoot this fella?" the man with the badge asked.

"Yes," Dane answered.

"Want to tell me what it's all about?"

Babbit laughed, another coughing, blood-spraying laugh. "Sheriff, don't blame my friend here," he said. "If he hadn't killed me, I would have killed him. Fact is, he done me a favor. This way, at least, I ain't goin' to hang."

"That's right, Sheriff," one of the witnesses said.

"The fella on the floor drew first. It was a pure case of self-defense."

"You shoulda seen it, Sheriff," another offered. "It was the fastest thing I ever seen in my life."

The sheriff sighed and looked at Dane. "Did you have to bring your beef to my town?"

"Sorry, Sheriff, but this is where I caught up with him," Dane said. He nodded toward Babbit. "This is Nathan Babbit. You'll find paper on him in your office. I'll be wantin' a receipt from you for him."

"You a bounty hunter?"

"Why, Sheriff, don't you recognize him?" Babbit asked. His voice was weaker now, and racked with pain. "This here is Dane Calder. Me and him is old friends now. He's been after me for more'n a year."

"Calder?"

"I've heard of him," one of the fellas in the bar said.

"Boys, we're goin' to have some story to tell. We just seen Dane Calder in action," another said.

The sheriff held up his hand to silence the crowd reaction.

"I've heard of you, Calder," he said. "They say you're a hard man, but I've never heard tell of you shootin' one of your quarry in the back. All right, I'll give you your receipt, but then I want you to leave. If there's anything I don't want in this town, it's a gunfighter...even one that's on the side of the law. Do you understand what I'm saying."

"I'll be on my way, Sheriff, soon as you give me the receipt," Dane said.

The sheriff went over to the bar. "Ed, you got a tablet and pencil?"

The bartender reached under the bar and came up with the items.

"Your name Nathan Babbit like he says?" the sheriff asked Babbit.

"That's it, Sheriff. Nathan Babbit, with two b's," Babbit said. He snorted. "Wouldn't want my name misspelled on the tombstone."

"Received of Dane Calder, the body of one Nathan Babbit, wanted man, killed in a fair gunfight in the town of Rio Lobo. Signed, Sheriff Gus Thorsall," the sheriff said, speaking aloud as he wrote. He tore the page off the tablet and handed it to Dane. "Will that do you?"

"That will do just fine, Sheriff. Thank you," Dane answered, folding the piece of paper and putting it in his shirt pocket. He started toward the door.

"Calder, wait a minute!" Babbit called to Dane. "You ain't goin' to just leave me like this, are you? I got a pain in my gut somethin' awful. Why didn't you shoot me in the head or the heart and get it over with?"

"I shot you just where I wanted to shoot you, Babbit," Dane said.

"Well, finish me off now, you bastard!" Babbit shouted. "Don't you leave me like this!"

Dane started for the door again.

"Think about the Indian girl."

Dane remained rooted to the floor, though his hand began to move slowly toward his pistol.

"That's it!" Babbit said. "That's it! Shoot me! Yes, go ahead! Shoot me!"

Dane sighed and let his arm drop down to his side. He started once more toward the door.

"Don't you want me to die? What's the matter? Are you showing yella?"

Dane pushed through the bat-wing doors, walked by Babbit's dead horse, and climbed on his own animal for the long ride back to Coyote Springs. After more than a year of burning, the fire in his gut was out.

A LOOK AT:

SLAUGHTER AT REBEL RIDGE

When evil dominates Rebel Ridge, there's only one person to call on for help.

In the dusty frontier town of Rebel Ridge, Sheriff Jesse Loman rules with an iron fist, exploiting the local populace through unjust taxes and a corrupt legal system. His gang of outlaw deputies ensures his dominance, staging mock trials and sentencing innocents to the gallows while protecting their own.

But when chaos grips Rebel Ridge, hope arises in the form of a legendary bounty hunter. Renowned for his unwavering principles, Dane Caulder reluctantly steps in to free the town from Jesse's grasp, pitting himself against corrupt deputies in a deadly showdown.

Can Dane deliver the long-awaited justice that the oppressed town of Rebel Ridge yearns for—or will its chance at peace be slaughtered once and for all?

AVAILABLE NOW

ABOUT THE AUTHOR

Robert Vaughan sold his first book when he was nineteen. That was several years and nearly five-hundred books ago. Since then, he has written the novelization for the mini-series Andersonville, as well as wrote, produced, and appeared in the History Channel documentary Vietnam Homecoming.

Vaughan's books have hit the *NYT* bestseller list seven times. He has won the Spur Award, the Porgie Award in Best Paperback Original, the Western Fictioneers Lifetime Achievement Award, the Readwest President's Award for Excellence in Western Fiction, and is a member of the American Writers Hall of Fame and a Pulitzer Prize nominee.

He is also a retired army officer, helicopter pilot with three tours in Vietnam, who has received the Distinguished Flying Cross, the Purple Heart, The Bronze Star with three oak leaf clusters, the Air Medal for valor with 35 oak leaf clusters, the Army Commendation Medal, the Meritorious Service Medal, and the Vietnamese Cross of Gallantry.